The Touch

By Ron Chocolate

PublishAmerica
Baltimore

ISBN: 1-4241-8428-2
PUBLISHED BY PUBLISHAMERICA, LLLP
www.publishamerica.com
Baltimore

Printed in the United States of America

"For from within, out of the heart of men, proceed evil thoughts, adulteries, fornications, murders" (Mark 7:21).

It was five in the evening and Kevin was on his way to his last store. He had already done six and he never before done that many in one day. He had been working since six in the morning and his nerves were failing him now. He felt like he would explode if someone flipped the wrong switch and he wouldn't even hesitate to think about the consequences. If the police showed up Kevin would have fought them also and wouldn't have stopped until one of them shot him. That way he would be sure that his family would be taken care of instead of him going to jail. He was sure that they would receive at least a half a million just from his company. Then there would be more coming from the insurance company. Kevin would very much wish for his own death before he sat in jail and did nothing the rest of his life. He thought that jail was pointless and would amount to nothing. Those who did wrong should pay for it and be killed not thrown into a room with another man and be fed three meals a day. That would seem like paradise to some people, and it was all free so there would be nothing for them to worry about. If Kevin had a time machine one of the first things he would do would be to go back in time and slap the person who invented the jailing system. All it did was allow people who deserved nothing something and that was what Kevin hated about it. If they were to gain anything it would have to come after their death for it to please Kevin. What irritated him even more than that was the reason they jailed people instead of killing them. God, but that will come later.

This day was one day Kevin wished things had gone right instead of wrong. Well, he wished that every day was a good one, but this one was one of the worst. He didn't even have a chance to get his coffee in the morning and he barely had time to get something to eat. What he got to eat was cold and he almost threw it right back up after he had gotten it down. He had to drink almost an entire gallon of water to keep it down. He then walked outside to find even more dilemmas. At first his van acted as if it didn't want to start. He had to work on it for about thirty minutes, but luckily he finally got it running. That was about the only good thing that happened. One of his sons had forgotten to put the trash in the can and a dog had gotten to it. He would have just left it there, but he couldn't allow it to just sit there and get nasty. He moved as quickly as he could and picked up the mess. Then he tried to get back to his car and get going, but before he had made it he got a call on his cell phone. It was his boss. He was angry with him because he was getting complaints on the job, but Kevin really didn't care at the time. Kevin was too tired to listen to him and even if he hadn't been he still wouldn't have paid him any mind. He was an annoying monster who had nothing better to do with his life, but yell at someone. Kevin felt sorry for his children.

After he finally got his car running, he drove down the street and then noticed that he had forgotten his map; he had to drive all the way back home and quickly found it and that took about an hour. Now he was even more behind. He then drove in the wrong direction and he quickly had to back track to make up for lost time. Soon he got on the right road and got going. He had about fifty miles to go before he got to his first store, but as long as he got there he wouldn't mind when.

He didn't feel like putting up with the costumers or the employees. He wished that he could somehow just make them say only what he wanted to hear and that would be that they didn't need him to do much on their store. There wasn't much that could be done about foolish people. You could either ignore them and act as if they didn't bother you, or you had to communicate and act as if you like them. Kevin found the first one a lot easier to do and usually did it. Every once in a while he would come in contact with someone who would just want to get on his nerves for what seemed like no reason. It was as if he had pulled some kind of switch inside of his head and it made them hate Kevin. Though this was one of the worst days of his life, he was happy that he hadn't run into any of those kinds of people and he was able to ignore all of the people who he had come in contact with. Well at least most of them.

Kevin was known for his temper. It's not that he had a terrible temper or anything, but he sometimes had difficulty keeping it under control. He had outbursts of rage when he was younger. One minute he would just be sitting there and the next he was screaming about something and his mother would have to sing to him to calm him down. Soon, as he grew older, he learned more and more about what caused his anger and he taught himself how to deal with it. He did this by asking himself if that person was worth him going to jail over, and once he did that he usually didn't even want to hurt the person anymore; in fact, he usually couldn't make any sense of why he was trying to fight them in the first place. It would all seem pointless to him then and he tried to just let it go. Sometimes the other person wouldn't want to just forget about it and Kevin would serenely and respectfully tell them the reason why it really didn't matter. If that didn't work Kevin would just have to use some force and put an end to all of it. He didn't have many acquaintances and that was because he didn't trust anyone. He had trouble trusting his wife and he didn't even trust God anymore so he didn't see why he should trust people whom he scarcely knew. He just made up his mind to forget about all of his old friends and live life as if they had never been there. That wasn't very hard because almost all of his friends from high school were either dead or in jail. He hadn't really hung out with people of good quality when he was younger. He used to think that was just a part of being in school and he didn't let it bother him. Besides it was worth that fun, right?

He had a gentle heart (well, for the most part) and would do just about anything for his family, maybe even murder someone. He had never had to decide between the two, but he was sure that he would choose the latter instead of his family. People are going to destroy themselves anyways, is what he always thought, so why not just help the process and protect his family? What did other people matter to him? He had never killed anyone, and though there were many he wanted to kill he could never bring himself to do something like that. But, there was that one time.

It was the day his father decided that life wasn't worth living anymore and that he was going to kill everyone he had ever loved so no one else could ever adore them. Kevin was fortunate that his father thought it would have been a blessing to kill him and that it would please him to see his son perish away into nothing here on Earth. At first no one knew who was doing all of the killings. There bodies would just show up one day and there wasn't any explanation about how or why they had been killed. Mark, Kevin's father, had killed five people and no one had any indication that he had done it except his wife, Paula. She had heard Mark on the phone and had seen pictures of all of the victims and she knew they were all of Mark's ex-girlfriends. She went to the police and told them what she knew, but before they could find Mark, he vanished and wasn't seen for a year. Kevin was having his tenth birthday and Paula and the cops, who were guarding her and Kevin, got drunk. They were running around having a good time and didn't even notice Mark, walking into the house. One of the cops asked Mark if he wanted some beer and Mark took the bottle and stuffed it down his throat. The other policeman had seen this and he tried to get his gun, but he couldn't see straight and Mark took his gun from him and shot him in his head. Then Mark went into the kitchen and got a knife. Paula was inside of her bedroom sleeping and didn't even hear him approaching. He stabbed her in her chest three or four times until he was sure that she was dead and then he hacked off her head. Once he had gotten it off, he lifted it up into the air and then threw it out the window. Kevin had heard the gunshot and walked to his mother's room to see if she was all right. He had seen everything that Mark had done to his mother, and had stood there in astonishment not knowing what he should do. Mark then laid the knife down next to Paula's body

6

and walked past Kevin as if he was an effigy. He didn't even glance slightly at him. Once he had left the room, Kevin ran over to his mother's body and cried for a moment. Then he picked up the knife and chased after his father. Mark was almost out of the house when Kevin called his name. He stopped for a moment but then he continued to walk away. Kevin called him once more and when he didn't get a response he threw the knife at his father striking him in his back and paralyzing him for life. Kevin only wished he had killed him.

Kevin was listening to the radio as he drove down the interstate. He had an atrocious voice and would never sing in front of people, but loved to sing whenever he was alone. He was ready for the day to be over with so he could get home to see his family, but it looked as if that wouldn't be happening anytime soon. There was a traffic jam and he couldn't go anywhere because he didn't know any other way to get around to his store. Kevin hated being stuck in traffic and blamed it on the other people. He wished that they could just learn to drive in a straight line and just allow the other person to cross over when they needed to. It took him almost an hour to get through the jam and he was very irate by then. He would have cursed and gotten mad with himself, but then he remembered what his grandfather had always told him: "Everything has a bright side and you just have to look for it. You should never let the bad things get you down, sonny." In fact, that was the last thing Kevin could remember him ever saying. The only good thing Kevin saw in this jumble was that Wal-Mart was open twenty-four hours a day and he didn't have to fret about being behind schedule.

He came into the parking lot around six-thirty. When he got out of the car he felt like he had no strength at all but he had made up his mind that he would finish his stores for the day. He was still agitated and he tried to calm himself down, because if he had another complaint from someone he would be fired. That was something he didn't want to happen. Sure he didn't make as much money as the job was worth and it wasn't all that grand of a job, but he liked it for some anonymous reason. He didn't want to have to try to find another career though he knew he would not find a career any worse than the army. The army was something he hated with a great passion. He had served in it for almost eighteen years, and had never once had an enjoyable day. Once he heard about the war that President Bush was sending the army to, he decided he should retire early and take his chances living a civilian life. Most of his family did not want to leave Germany, but his mind was made up and he couldn't stay there any longer. Kevin hoped that he would feel a little safer living in America, but once he got there he almost wished he hadn't.

Kevin walked over to the building and got a grocery cart to put his equipment in. He worked for a company called Serve Mart and installed their radios into the Wal-Mart stores and various other shop's displays. He loved installing them, but hated putting up with all of the people. There was one shop that he detested the most. Every time he got to that shop, he wanted to just skip it but he could not do that so he went in. There was a woman manager and he didn't know why but she loathed him. He tried to be nice but every time he came she just pissed him off. There was a rule that he followed because of the company that said he should wait five minutes and if they didn't bring him the material that he needed he would just get up and leave. He had been to that store three times before and each time she would just forget about him and he would leave. The last time he went he almost got into a fight with the woman.

"Hello, Miss, would you give me a quick moment of your time?" asked Kevin as politely as he could.

"Yes what do you want?" said the woman harshly.

"I would like to finally put up your display for you. If you don't mind."

"Well, why the hell haven't you put it up yet? I know you've been here at least five times."

"Miss, this has been the third time I've come here and twice before you wouldn't allow me to put up the display. I wouldn't mind if I could just get it over and done with."

"Well, there's no one stopping you."

"Yes, but I need the—"

The woman cut him off and then said, "You know I don't have time for this. Find the stuff yourself and put it up, since you're in such a hurry."

"I'm sorry but I don't do that."

"Well, then what do you do?"

"Miss, you can either get me the stuff or I'll leave and come back another time."

"Well, why are you still here then?"

"Miss, what is your problem?" said Kevin with an irritated tone.

"What?"

"WHAT IS YOUR PROBLEM?" Kevin said loudly and everyone in the store turned to look at him.

"I don't have a problem. You have the problem and if you do get out of my store I'm going to have the cops come and throw you out."

"Are you threatening me?"

"Did it sound like a threat?"

"You know what? I think I know what your problem is."

"What is it?"

"You don't like black people. Do you?"

"I don't have—"

Kevin threw his tablet on the counter and cut her off. "No, I don't even want to hear it. I've been in here twice now and I don't want you to do anything but give me the stereos to put in the display. Is that too much to ask or are you so old and broken down to get off of your lazy a...butt and get me the things." After Kevin said this, the woman grabbed the closest thing she could find and smacked him in the face. Kevin quickly retaliated and soon they were fighting. The crowd in the store broke them up and soon the police came. That was the only one of Kevin's complaints that he didn't disgust himself for. In fact he thought that he had given the woman just what she needed. He never thought too much about race, but he didn't understand why anyone would want to judge a person by the color of their skin. Why wouldn't you hope that everyone you met was a well and nice person? By looking at someone's skin and then judging them you just caused more problems that could have been avoided. The world would be such a better place if everyone could either become one color or learn to live without thinking or seeing other people as bad or wrong.

After Kevin finished loading his things into the cart, he locked his car and went into the store. He would usually leave his car unlocked but he had never been to this town before. This store was one of his new ones and he knew it would take him at least an hour or two to finish, but he wanted it out of the way. He hated how his boss would just throw stores on him at the last minute. He could not refuse because then he would either be fired or something would make him give in anyways. It didn't matter all that much though because he really loved his job. He didn't understand why he loved it so much. It was just a feeling he got deep down inside that made him blissful. He could have been working for hours and wouldn't even feel as if he was working. He would feel almost refreshed and almost wished there was still more work to be done. The only downfall was being away from his family for so long. He hoped he would never have to be gone for as long as he had before. That seemed to be when all of the terrible things happened.

He did his work in the electronics and automotive sections of the store. He wished that they would have placed the two of them relatively close to each other. It's not that he was too lazy to walk from one place to the other or anything, but in almost every store he had been in he would have to walk from one side of the store to the other. If he every forgot something he would have to walk all the way to the other side and then come back. He thought of bringing one of his children with him to do the walking for him, but when he put it into action it didn't seem to work out at all. They would usually forget about him and he would end up doing it himself anyways.

He walked into the electronics section first and asked for the manager. The cashier told him that the manager was on his break and would be back in five minutes so Kevin waited. He hated to just sit down and waste time doing nothing so he started to take out his things so he could be ready to work when he showed up. He walked over to the display and finished getting ready. One of the stereos was on and there were people talking about the world's current events.

"There was a train wreck this evening," said the man on the radio. "Four people were inside of the car that was hit and only one of them survived. He said that they were trying to beat the train and they thought they would make it, but as you can see that plan didn't work out as well as they thought it would. What is this world coming to? Children these day are crazy. Am I right?" There were voices in the background that yelled yes and then he started to talk again. "In other news Bush put the Iraq government back into power. Bush and the rest of our government think that our troops will remain over there for another two to three years or at least until they believe everything will be safe. I don't think that the troops being over there will make much of a difference. I think it might just make things worse for the Iraq government. We would love to hear what you think about this. Call 640-9758 and tell us what you think. Well, I also have a letter here that I want to read to you. It is from somebody named Believer. I got this in the mail earlier this morning. He or she somehow got this letter to us and it's about the man that was decapitated a few day ago. Well, here I'll just read it to you:

"'Dear world, I have lived in America my entire life. I have seen things that weren't all that right but I guess they had to be done. There have been many wars over the years and the schools insist on us learning history so one day we might learn from our mistakes and become a better union, but it seem to me that it's only getting worse. The United States of America is supposed to be the greatest place on the face of the Earth. In other words we seem to have all of the power and what we say goes. I see that as a dictatorship and isn't that the one thing we seem to be fighting in Iraq. America went to war without the help of the UN, but now it seems that we need their help and that it was foolish of us to do anything without everyone else's help. I believe in God and I think that this is the end and soon we will destroy ourselves. I wrote this hoping to try to change our fate but that's impossible and there is nothing I can do about the end that will and is coming. All I can do is pray and I hope something will help to change what we have already begun. I hope everyone has heard about that man that was killed in such a crucial way that I wouldn't even mention much of it in this letter. He was an innocent person that just found himself in the wrong place at the wrong time. That man was killed for no reason. We wouldn't negotiate and they weren't going to play games with us. I don't think we should have negotiated but we should have done anything other than just sitting and watching him died. What if that was someone who was close to you. I'm sure you would want somebody to do something, but instead we expected him to just sit there and die for the well-being of America the great. What makes it so great? I don't see anything better about America that puts us ahead of any other country. Bush sent the troops, but I bet he won't go and fight. He would never do a thing like that, because there just a slight chance that he and his troops will not be coming back. I...'" Kevin had been listening to the radio and didn't notice the manager trying to get his attention.

"Hello, I heard you wanted to see me," said the manager, tapping Kevin on the shoulder.

"Oh, yes. I was just listening to this thing on the radio."

"Yeah, all this is just a big mess."

"Yes, I'm just glad I got out before all this got started."

"What do you mean? Were you in the military or something?"

"Yes, I was."

"So why did you get out? You could have been over there trying to make things better. I hope you weren't afraid or anything."

"I just didn't want to go to war and fight for a cause that I didn't believe in. I don't see any reason why I should have been afraid."

"It must be tough for all of them over there in Iraq fighting, and all they want to do it be at home with their family."

"Yes." Kevin paused for a moment. As much as he wanted to talk to someone about what was happening, he more eagerly wanted to get to work so he could be with his family. "Do you have the stuff for this display?"

"Yes, I brought it with me. Is that all you need?"

Kevin looked at the basket and was amazed to find all of the things he needed in there. It usually took awhile for the people to cooperate with him, correctly.

"That's all I need. I'll put this in here and be on my way."

"Hey, are you going to come here every two weeks or what?"

"I should be around here just about every two weeks."

"What happened to the other man that used to come here? I hope he got fired, because he only came every other month and things would break down and just stay that way until he came."

Kevin looked up at the man and thought for a moment and then said, "He tried his best to come here every two weeks, but coming here to Texas all the way from Mississippi every two weeks is a big hassle."

"Well, if I had known that I would have been a lot nicer to him. I wouldn't want to come all the way from Mississippi every two weeks. I guess we should thank God for you."

"Or, you could just thank me." The manager looked at Kevin as if he wanted to say something, but thought twice about it and left him so he could get on with his work. It really wasn't that difficult of a job, but it just took time to make sure he put everything in its right place. While he worked he liked to hum to himself but today he didn't because he always stopped when people were around. Every time he thought he was alone someone else would come over and bother him so he just went on working without humming. There was one thing that really troubled him about working at Wal-Mart, and that was that everyone always asked you where to find something or for some kind of help. Kevin would always be in the middle of putting something together when someone would ask him: where are the radios, where can I find some electric tape, or can you help me with something, sir? Every time someone would ask him one of these questions he would tell them that he did not work for Wal-Mart. Most of them would just leave but some of them just had to start something, and they would say, "then why are you here working on the display?" He would just look at them like they were dense and then he'd go back to work. That's how he had gotten another one of his complaints.

He remembered that day more than any of the others because his wife had almost left him for that one. He was just humming to himself like any other day and a woman came up to him. She was very attractive and she looked like an angel to Kevin, but he didn't believe in cheating on his wife. She was once just as beautiful until they had children. Kevin believed that children really helped you to age faster

13

than you should. When ever he got the temptation to cheat on his wife, he always asked himself if his wife was still young and beautiful would he choose this woman over her. The answer always turned out to be no. Kevin had never seen a woman as beautiful as his wife had once been and he thought that he would never see anything that beautiful ever again.

The woman had asked Kevin about how she should install a specific kind of VCR in her household. She said that she wanted to make sure that it was done right and would appreciate a professional installment. He told her that there were a lot of factors involved and that she should get an electrician to come over and look at it for her. She said that she didn't know any good quality electricians that weren't expensive and that she was sure he could come over do just as good of a job anyone else. Though she played the part of an innocent, helpless woman, Kevin had been in the army long enough to know how to read a person's real intentions. Once he was sure of what she wanted, he told her that he was married and didn't need any temptation in his life to make him do the wrong thing. All she said was that it couldn't be wrong if you paid for it. He said that she should leave and that he didn't have time for such things, but for some reason she wouldn't take no for an answer. She quickly reached down and grabbed Kevin's crouch. He pushed her back and told her that she should find someone else because he wasn't interested. Then she ripped her shirt and exposed most of her breasts but not all of them and screamed that he had tried to seduce her. It all made no sense to Kevin and he just went back to work. The manager of the store called the police and when they got there Kevin told them what had happened. They asked him why they thought she would do something like this and he told them that he didn't know, and that he had never seen the woman before in his life.

The police didn't know who to believe so they arrested Kevin and took him down to the police station. Soon they called his wife and she came as fast as she could. She didn't believe that Kevin would do something like that and told the police so. She said that he was a good man and would do nothing to hurt his family. The police really didn't have any evidence to keep him in jail for long and the camera hadn't recorded anything that he happened so they let Kevin go. Then he and his wife went home and he took the week off. Soon the investigators found Kevin's prints on the part of the shirt that had been ripped, and he told them that they were there because he had pushed her away. The police believed him but his wife didn't. She saw the woman and she knew that that woman looked almost exactly like she used to when they had gotten married. Kevin told her he would never do a thing like that but his wife wouldn't listen to what he had to say. She was full of jealousy and couldn't believe what she was seeing. All she could think about was how she had lost her beauty and her place taken away from her. Kevin tried over and over to tell her that it wasn't true, but she still left him with the children that same night. Kevin didn't know where she had gone and he almost forced himself to go to God for an answer, but then he thought better of it. Or at least what he thought was better.

It took the police another day or so to get a confession out of the woman. At first she was confused about where she was and what she was doing. The police couldn't find her in their computer and had no clue of who she was. She told them that the last thing she remembered was taking some kind of pill and then passing out. The police decided to test her and see if she had taken some kind of drug and found out that she had. Soon her name came back to her and then she remembered what she had done and went to apologize to Kevin and his wife. After she apologized Kevin's wife came back to him and he continued to tell her that he was telling the truth the entire time. She soon gave in and told him that she believed him, but that really wasn't the truth. Even though there was a confession from the woman Samantha, Kevin's wife, almost hoped that she had been telling the truth before. She thought that would have been for the best and would have saved both her and Kevin a lot of time.

Kevin finished putting in the displays in the entertainment section and went over to the electronics to put in the displays over there. He had to wait another five minutes for the manager to come and give him the things, but once he got them Kevin quickly got to work. After he had finished that he had to go and get his papers signed. He really hated this part of his job. The people would always tell him to wait a second and he ended up waiting for almost fifteen or twenty minutes. Today the person that he needed to sign his papers was filling in for someone else and wouldn't be able to help him until another five or so minutes. So he decided to look around the store and see if he could find something for his son. He had three of them; one was fifteen, one was twelve and the other was six. The older two wouldn't be happy with a cheap toy or anything so he thought he would just buy them a video game that they could all play together. He walked over to the game section of the store and looked at all the games. Most of the games they already had and they had all of the systems. They had the Xbox, the Playstation 2, and the Gamcube. He just didn't know what to buy them so he just got the newest game that he could find. This game was called *The Legend of Zelda, Four Swords*. He just hoped that they didn't have it already. He and his children didn't get along well most of the time. The oldest was always working out and going out with his friends and rarely spoke to him, the second oldest was always talking about something that never seemed important and everyone was always telling him to shut up, and the youngest always wanted to do whatever the older two were doing and when he couldn't he would cry. It seem almost pointless to Kevin to try to please all of them.

Kevin bought the game and started to walk back over the automotive section where he had to get his papers signed. As he walked someone stopped him. He didn't know the man but he acted as if he knew him. He was wearing very plain clothes and looked almost as if he was homeless. Kevin would have thought that he was if it hadn't been for the keys that hung out of his pocket.

"Hey, how are you?" said the stranger, reaching his hand out to shake hands with Kevin.

"I'm good, but I don't see why you would care?" said Kevin, just looking past him and not even thinking about shaking his hand. Kevin had learned over the years that it was pointless to talk to strangers for no reason. They would almost always want something from you and soon try to take advantage of you. Kevin trusted no one but his family and he didn't have time to add anyone to the list. He was certain that this man wanted something and Kevin had made up his mind not to give it to him. Even if he had to break his nose to make him go away.

"I want your help with something."

"And what is that?"

The man paused for a moment and he looked around. He had a troubled look on his face as if he was thinking of what he should say. "I'll meet you outside, and then we can talk."

"I don't even know you, why would I want to help you?" Kevin pushed him out of his way and he started to walk past him but he grabbed him and pulled him back over in front of him. He had a very concerned look on his face and it almost scared Kevin. He thought for a moment that this man was insane and might want to kill him. If it came to that Kevin was well prepared to fight him.

"I don't think you can just walk away like that. I want to speak with you and I think you really would like to hear this," said the man, looking Kevin right in the eyes.

"I don't want anything to do with you. If you don't let me go I will call security," said Kevin, pulling away from him.

"Okay, just go, but we'll talk later. My names John, John Abbgies. Please remember that."

"Are you gay or something? I don't need to know your name." Then Kevin just walked away and didn't give John another chance to try to talk to him. Kevin started to walk back to the automotive section watching his back the entire time. He kept thinking that John might jump out at him and try to force him to listen to him. Kevin was relieved to find that he had made it to the automotive section without seeing John again. The woman behind the counter told him that she was sorry she had made him wait and he quickly got his papers signed and he headed for the exit. He was happy to get up out of the store and he quickly got his equipment and took off before he had a chance to see John again. He looked at his watch and saw that it was already nine. He usually would have just gone to a hotel and his company would have paid for it, but this time he didn't make reservation because he had planned to be at home by now. If it hadn't been for the wreck earlier, he would have been done with this store a long time ago and may have been home by now.

He checked his map and saw that he only lived an hour away from the last store he had just gotten finished with. He told himself that he could make it there and the only obstacle that was in his way was forcing himself to stay awake. He looked at his clock again and noticed that it was unusual for him to stay up this late, but he figured that he could do it. Well, he used to when he was younger but nowadays Samantha seemed as if she didn't care much for sex or any other kind of late-night activity any more so he just tried to get on without it. That really didn't bother him, because he was forty years old and didn't love having sex as much as he used to. One reason was that it was what caused him to have children. It's not that he did not love his children, but he had to grow up once he had them and that was the only reason he joined the army. If it wasn't for his children he might have gone to college.

Kevin hated driving at night, especially when he was alone and there weren't many cars around. When there were other cars out he would imagine that they were all in a race or something, and that would help him to stay awake. Kevin had been falling asleep and he almost hit a car as it came speeding by him just as he started to drift into the other lane. He luckily woke up just in time to turn the wheel and save his life. After that Kevin was in a stage of shock and couldn't imagine trying to go to sleep. His senses were like those of a cat and he tried to think of things that would keep him awake. Soon another car from behind Kevin. They must have been in some kind of hurry or they were drunk, because they didn't seem to notice the other car coming towards them. The car tried to pass Kevin and thought that he would make it. Kevin knew that he wouldn't and he quickly pulled on the brakes so he could avoid the crash. Kevin closed his eyes so he wouldn't have to see what happened. Soon he heard the scratching of metal. His mind started to hurt from the intensity of the sound and Kevin had to put his hands on his head to try to keep it from exploding. Of course, that wouldn't have helped if it was really going to explode, but there wasn't much of anything else he could do. Soon the pain started to diminish and Kevin put his hands down. When he opened his eyes everything looked normal and there wasn't any trace of there ever being any kind of crash. He quickly closed his eyes and reopened them. He was hoping that his eyes were just playing tricks on him, but he found the same results in front of him. There was no crash. There wasn't any kind of tire marks on the ground or anything. Everything looked peaceful and in tranquilly. If there had been a crash it had somehow disappeared and there was no trace of it having ever been there.

Kevin decided that he must have fallen asleep and imaged it. Once he talked himself into believe that that was the truth he took off back down the road. While he was driving a car came by and passed him again. This one was going twice as fast as the other one and almost knocked Kevin off the road. Kevin could understand that people had to get where they were going and didn't want to be late, but he always made sure that he drove under the speed limit. There had been a time when he wasn't worried about the speed limit and he would drive as fast as he wanted to, but he had reason for changing his ways. His brother was eighteen years old when he died from a car wreck. He wasn't drunk, but he was in a rush. He had been going twenty miles over the speed limit and ran into the back of a drunk driver's car. The drunk driver claimed that he thought he had seen a stop sign and so he stopped. All that did was prove that he was drunk and make Kevin hate him twice as much. The drunk driver lived around where Kevin lived but he could never remember his name. He knew that he went to the church Kevin used to go to and sang in the choir, but he never talked to him after his brother's death. He had tied to forget the man and move on with his life, but he could never forget his face. If he was to ever go back to the church he didn't know if he could keep himself from killing him, but that didn't matter because by the time of his brother's death he didn't believe in attending church and after his death he swore that he would never go back again.

As Kevin drove down the road he noticed that John was still on his mind. Now he thought maybe he should have waited and talked to him, but then he thought maybe he could have been insane or something and just have wanted to kill him or something. Either way it was too late now and he would never know what he wanted. He tried to think of someplace where he may have seen John before but he could not recall ever seeing him. He thought as hard as he could and came up with nothing. He figured that if he had seen him it would come to him later and that he should try to relax so he turned on the radio. He went through all of the FM stations but he couldn't pick up anything. Soon he just gave up and started to think of something to sing. It is funny how when you hear a song that you like you'll always want to sing to it but once it's gone you don't even care for it all that much. He tried to think of music, but his mind continued to drift off towards other things. No matter how hard he tried he couldn't focus on anything. Soon he just stopped thinking and continued driving down the vacant road.

As he drove he continued to become more and more restive and soon he couldn't drive any more. He decided to just stop for now at one of the gas stations and call in his stores while he rested so he wouldn't forget about them later. He didn't use his cell phone because he didn't want them to call him on his phone when ever they wanted him so he went over to the pay phone to called them in. He had done six stores that day and it took him awhile to call them all in. Usually he would only do about four but he had been sick and gotten behind so he did six to make sure that he wouldn't stay behind on his stores. Once he was finished he went into the store and bought a Doctor Pepper to help keep him awake. He would have preferred some coffee but their coffee machine was broken. He thought that was weird because it just happened to be broken when he came by to get something to drink. He knew that he could have come in looking for something else and the coffee machine would have been fine. He had to pay two dollars for the drink, but at the time he didn't care at all. He knew that it was a rip off and he should have walked away, but he needed the drink and he was sure that they needed the money. He walked back to his car having drunk most of the drink and got inside feeling a little better.

It was twelve now and Kevin was still about thirty minutes away. He really had not gotten very far in the two hours that he had been driving. He had dozed of on the side of the road about every five minutes and he ended up not making any progress at all. He wasn't worried about how long it would take him to get home because it was

Friday and he didn't have to work tomorrow, so he decided to just take his time and get home when he got there. He tried the radio again but there still wasn't any signal. *Where am I?* thought Kevin as he drove. He didn't know of any place that didn't have a radio station. He should have been on the intersection that would have taken him straight to his home. He had driven on that road hundreds of times, but not once was there no radio signals on any of the stations. It didn't make any sense to him so he pulled over to look at his map.

He looked at the road that he should have been on but he didn't see anything that looked like the things he saw around him. Everything looked unfamiliar and Kevin looked twice to make sure that it wasn't just the night and his eyes changing the scene. Since he had driven on the road for many years, one day he took the time to draw things on the map that he had always seen on the roads every time he drove through them. He couldn't see any road that matched or connected to the road he was on now. This road just seemed to appear out of nowhere. All of the roads around this area he had driven on and this one wasn't anywhere on the map. About three feet up the road from him was a sign that was black and blank. It was nowhere on his map and he was certain that he was lost. Kevin thought maybe if he got out and looked at the sign it would help him to figure out where he was. So he drove up beside it and looked out his window and still he could see nothing. He had to know if there was something there so he got out and looked again. He still couldn't see anything, but he was sure that something was moving on the sign. He didn't know what it was, but it seemed to squirm back and forth and it blended with the exact color of the sign.

Kevin was apprehensive about touching it at first, but then he decided that he would rather know what was there and face the danger instead of just walking away. He slowly reached his hand out and put it on the bottom of the sign. Then he started to slide his hand up the sign towards the creature that was unknown. Soon his hand came in contact with it and he almost jumped. It felt tremendously cold and Kevin thought for a moment that his hand had been immovable, but he quickly pulled it back to make sure. Once he was sure that his hand was okay and it was safe to touch it Kevin reached up again and grabbed the creature. It didn't seem to even notice Kevin and continued on as if he wasn't there. Then something came over Kevin that he could not explain. Something was telling him to just reach out and pull the creature off of the sign and look at it. So that's what he did.

In his hand he held some kind of black glob. Kevin didn't know what to make of it and he didn't know whether he should be afraid or not. It didn't look like it was harmful, but Kevin had learned a long time ago not to judge a book by its cover. He stared at the glob for a moment longer and then he started to poke it. His finger would just go inside of it and there would seem to be no kind of response. Soon Kevin grew bored with his new find and he threw it onto the ground as he walked back to his car.

He should have been watching his back, because then he might have noticed the glob behind him transforming into a new state. By the time Kevin did notice the glob it was too late and he couldn't react. He fell on his face as something bit into his ankle. Quickly he turned himself around so he could see his opponent and was astonished at what he found. The glob had somehow transformed itself into a snake. It was still black, but green venom could be seen dripping from its mouth as it took another bite into Kevin's leg. He wanted to scream, but he couldn't feel much of anything because of the venom. Kevin felt helpless, but he still managed to knock the snake off of him. Then he got to his feet and limped towards his car. He didn't know what he was going to do once he got into the car, but at the time that seemed like his only hope. He thought he was going to make it there for a moment.

Soon Kevin could feel his feet leaving the ground and he was paralyzed with surprise. He didn't know what was happening and he could not stop it. His body just continued to go higher and higher into the sky. He looked up to see if there was anything pulling him up but he found nothing. It was as if he had an invisible string attached to him and he was in some kind of magic show. The only thing that bothered him was than he had no idea of how the trick was going to ended. He didn't know if he was ever going to stop or if he was already dead and he was just going up to wherever he belonged. The thought of that terrified Kevin. He had thrown God away and forgotten about him so if he was ascending into the sky that could only mean that God was the truth and he would soon be punished. Though Kevin was petrified, he soon forgot about it and remembered what was below him.

Earth. Gravel. Dirt. What ever you want to call it, came flying towards Kevin as he fell. He didn't know what he had done to make it happen, but all of a sudden he just started to fall and there was once again nothing he could do. He felt his body starting to feel again, but that would not help any if he couldn't stop himself from falling. It seemed that the more he tried the faster he fell, and soon he noticed it was inevitable. If he had been a Christian he would have prayed, but instead he just screamed and cried as he got closer and closer. Soon he saw something coming into view. At first all he could see was the black and then he saw the snake. It was a hundred times bigger than it was before and looked twice as hungry. There was nothing Kevin could do, other than scream, as the snake devoured him and he went into the obscurity below.

Kevin opened his eyes to discover himself sitting in his car. It was as if he had never left and everything seemed ordinary. Kevin looked around in shock and he couldn't believe what was happening. He closed his eyes again and counted to ten to try to calm himself down. He had never done this before but had heard that it helped and it did. Once Kevin was sure of his atmosphere, he was going to get out of his car and inhale in some kind of fresh air when a hole appeared on his head. It wasn't that immense of a hole and he would have never noticed it if blood hadn't come dripping out of it. He quickly looked in the mirror to see the abrasion and when he couldn't, he grabbed some tissue from underneath his chair and wiped his head. By then the hole was gone and the blood had stopped saturating.

Kevin couldn't remember what happened next, but when he opened his eyes he was looking at his map again. He looked around for any sign of blood or anything that would have proven that what he had experienced was genuine but there was nil. He didn't know what to think and soon he gave up trying to figure things out. If there wasn't any proof then it must not have happened and that was all Kevin could say. He didn't believe in supernatural beings or things like that so it was either there or not and nothing else. He told himself that it must have just been a dream and he should look past it and make it home before something authentic happened to him. Now that his mind was made up he went back to his map.

He looked around on his map to see where he should have been and he saw something that reminded him of the road to his home. There was a gravestone that was halfway to his home and it always caught his eyes as he drove by it. On the gravestone there was a cross that had a snake coming up around it. Once he had seen some workers trying to remove the grave. They had it tied up to a truck and as the truck pulled back and tried to remove the grave the entire front bumper of the car was pulled off. The bumper hit one of the workers and his legs were ripped out from underneath him. After that Kevin never saw anyone trying to eradicate or even come in contact with the gravestone. He had once asked someone inside of the gas station closest to the grave how and why it was there. The man then told him this story.

"Hey, man," said Kevin to a man inside of a gas station.

"Yes, how many I help you?" answered the man as he put some money into the cash register.

"I want twenty dollars on pump two." The cashier took his money.

"There you go. I hope you have a good day."

"Hey, can I ask you something?"

"Yes, what?"

"What do you know about that cross out on the side of the road along the interstate? You know the one with the snake on it."

The man looked at Kevin for a moment and then looked away again. Kevin could tell that he was uncomfortable talking about the story, but if there was something that interesting about the grave Kevin just knew he had to find out and he wasn't going to let a man and what he felt stop him from finding out.

"Hey, I didn't mean to insult you or anything. I'm just curious."

Then man walked back over to Kevin and spoke with an angry look on his face.

"Are you a reporter or something, because I already sold my story to someone and they didn't even believe me. They made me look like an idiot. I don't want to show up in the science-fiction magazines again. It took almost a year for all of my friends and neighbors to stop laughing at me."

"No, I'm just curious. I don't mean to waste your time though. I wouldn't want anything bad to happen to you. I drive by the grave every day and was just curious that's all. I don't mean any harm." Kevin then started to walk away. The man didn't know why, but he felt as if he should tell Kevin about the grave. He seemed like an honest man.

"No, come back. I'll tell you. It might be better that you know anyways." He took a deep breath, while Kevin walked back over to him, and then he spoke. "There once was a possessed boy who had a great demon inside of him. He had the demon inside of him since he was born though no one knew exactly how it had gotten inside of him. From the moment he could walk he started to kill many people, but they never caught him because there was no proof. He would brag about it to his friend, who thought he was a god or something, and then when the police came around he would change. He sounded so innocent that they just couldn't believe that he had done it. He even went to church and withstood the power of God or at least it seemed. He lived with his grandma and she wouldn't believe that he had done anything to harm those people. Well, that's what she told the police, but not what she told her priest. She told him that her grandson was possessed and it got worse every time he killed someone. The priest came over to her house one day and he tried to help her grandson. At first he just prayed with him and his grandma, but a week later someone else died. The police were ready to kill the boy and the whole force went over to the house and demanded that the priest and the grandma would give them the boy so they could hang him. The priest asked them for just one more night to try to rid him of the demon and if that didn't work then they could do as they wished. So that night the priest tried to perform an exorcism but he didn't believe that it would really work. He didn't have the faith that was needed to expel the demon. Something made him try anyways. He walked into the room confident and with God, but he came out half dead and insane.

"He ran to the police and told them to come and kill the child as fast as they could. They all mocked him and asked him where his God had been when he tried to save the child. He told them to forget about God and just get rid of that child. They continued to laugh at him until they heard the explosion. The grandma's house was about a mile from the police department and it must have been a great explosion for them to hear it all the way down there. They all got into their cars and drove up to the house. The priest called every one else in the town once they had driven off. Then the priest walked back up to the house. Once he got there he found that everyone was dead. Every last one of them. It was the most horrible thing he had ever seen. There were bodies everywhere and they were so messed up that he couldn't even tell them apart. He couldn't tell if one person was female or male or even human for that fact. It took him awhile, but he finally made it up to the house. He was surprised to see that it was still there. He was almost sure that the boy had blown up the house and killed the grandmother, but the house was still there. The priest walked around to the back of the house to find more dead bodies and what had exploded. Somehow the child had blown up the entire back side of the house. I mean half of the house was gone. There was nothing. It looked entirely disintegrated. The grass around the back of the house and even part of the ground was gone. The priest had been holding himself back from throwing up but couldn't contain it any more when he looked down into the crater that the explosion had caused. There he found the entire police force dead. Their bodies weren't even intact. There were limbs everywhere and other things I really don't want to say. The priest wouldn't have even known that it was the police if it hadn't been for the badge he found in front of the crater.

"The grandma and the boy were still there out around the pond. The priest noticed them because the boy was screaming things and the grandma tried to calm him down but it wasn't working. The grandma looked as if she was trying to baptize him in the water, but soon the entire lake turned black and looked as if it was nothingness. This frightened the priest and he ran back up the hill and into the remainder of the house to hide. He found a table and quickly jumped under it and prayed. This was the first time he had even really prayed and it paid off. Soon he got a vision of a time he had come to the house before. He saw the grandma and the boy sitting at the table. The grandma was trying to talk to the boy but he wasn't listening. The priest wasn't worried about him because right behind them was something else of more importance. There was an angel.

"This was the greatest thing the priest had ever seen. It was magnificent, wonderful, indescribable, fantastic, marvelous, fabulous, and superb. He almost couldn't believe his eyes. There were no words to portray it. All you needed to do was imagine the greatest thing you can think of and that was what he saw. He would have traded anything in the world just to see what he had seen. He would have given his life and anything else he could have. If he had owned the world he would have given it up. There was just nothing he could imagine that would have been greater than this sight. The priest wanted to bow down and pray, but at the very moment he had thought about it the angel started to leave the room and walk down the hall. The priest didn't want to lose him and quickly started to follow. While he ran to catch up the only thought that was in his mind was that if an angel looked that beautiful, then how did God look?

"The priest followed the angel throughout the house and into a room in which he had never been. There, the angel stopped and smiled at him. That was an even greater sight than he had seen before and the shock of it almost made him faint. Soon the angel stopped and he opened the closet door. Then the angel kneeled down and pulled out a case of some kind. There was a lock on it and all the angel had to do was touch it to make it open. Inside was something the priest found would come in handy.

"When the priest had awoken, he had seen where the grandma had put her gun and he ran to get it. He quickly found the case and saw that the lock was still on it. He looked through the room for a key, but

27

there wasn't one. Then he remembered what the angel had done. He kneeled down on his knees and prayed with all of his heart and then touched the lock. It broke off as if it was a twig or something and then he grabbed the gun. By the time he had loaded that gun, the grandma and the boy had run into the woods. The priest followed them and soon he caught up with them. All he saw before he shot was the child biting into the grandma's hand. After the shot, the child lay down and disappeared into the ground and a cross come sprouting out. Then a snake crawled onto the cross. While it was crawling it turned into stone just like the cross. And it's been that way ever since."

There was a pause between the two of them and then Kevin spoke.

"That's messed up. How did you find out about it?"

"The priest was my great-grandfather."

Kevin made up his mind that he had somehow gotten on to the wrong road and he turned around. He couldn't figure out how he had made it all the way out here on a road he didn't even see on his map. He drove until he found a gas station and he got out to ask for directions. He had seen someone walking inside when he drove up to park, but now there wasn't a sign of anything or anyone. He banged on the door for a while, but no one came to answer. He screamed because he knew he had seen them. No one came. Kevin then kicked the door a couple of times and then yelled as many curse words as he could think of at the time. Soon he just went and got back into his car. He looked at the fuel meter and saw that it was half empty. He just hoped that would be enough for him to reach the next gas station. He rolled down the passenger side window and yelled one more curse word before driving off.

Kevin took the unfamiliar road all the way back until he found the Wal-Mart that he had just finished working at earlier. He pulled out his map and saw that he should have gone left instead of right on the road leading away from the store. His map also showed that the road he had just taken didn't even exist. He went into the Wal-Mart and bought a new map to look at and saw the same thing. He was frightened for a moment. He kept thinking that such a thing couldn't happen and he didn't believe in things like that. Then he made up his mind to go and look to see if the road was really there or if it wasn't. When he got there the road was gone. He looked at his watch and saw that it was almost two. *There must have been something there*, thought Kevin. He didn't think that he could have wasted all that time just sleeping in his car. He looked around to see if he still had the Doctor Pepper and found it under his seat. He had made up his mind. He was going to find out where the road had gone. He got out of his car and walked into the woods that had once been the mysterious road. He went down the woods for about a mile. He just went far enough to see if he could find a road anywhere in any direction. Once he thought he was far enough, he looked around in every direction and saw nothing. He started to walk back to his car when he looked around again and he saw the road. It was to the left of him and he couldn't believe how it had gotten there. It wasn't there a moment ago, but something had summoned it back.

Kevin was frightened even more now and he wanted to get to the bottom of it. He quickly ran back to his car and got in. He drove over to the spot where he had seen the road and saw that it was still there. He just stood there looking down the road. *I'll do this real quick, and then I go home*, thought Kevin and then he went into the forbidden road. As he drove he looked around to see if it was the same road and it wasn't. It was his road. It was the road that would take him to his home. The road he had been looking for before. He knew for sure once he got to the bumpy part of it that he hated. Once he got past that he saw all of the trees he had drown on his map. They stood out because there were hearts drawn on them with people's initials. Kevin wished his love had lasted as long as those hearts on the trees. That's mostly the reason he had drawn them down in the first place. He would give almost anything to go back in time and change all of the fights and all of the times he had a bad temper.

He didn't know how he had gotten on his road, but now he was happy that he would be home soon. He wondered if his wife would even be at home waiting for him. It seemed unlikely but a man can always hope for the best. He thought maybe if he hadn't left God his wife may not have left him. While she didn't really leave him corporeally, but psychologically they were divided. All of these things continued to build in his mind until his car stopped. Kevin was driving and it just killed over in the middle of the road. At first, Kevin didn't really notice but then a car drove by him and the man screamed something. Kevin was then wide-awake and he saw he wasn't moving. Just a few moments ago it had appeared to him that he had been driving and he hadn't felt anything when the car stopped. He got out and looked at the engine, but he didn't see anything wrong with it. His vehicle was a 1988 Astro Van, and it had broken down many times. One day he just got tired of it and bought a new engine and it hadn't broken down since, until now.

He got back in the car and tried to start the car again. After a few tries it started and Kevin started to drive again. He got a little farther down the road and then the car stopped. This time Kevin could feel it slowing down and he allowed it to roll forward after it had stopped and turned into the outside lane while putting on his brakes. He put his head on the steering wheel and took a deep breath. He told himself to stay calm and he got out to look under the hood once again. This time he still didn't see anything wrong with it. He just hoped that the car would start again and let him get home until it broke down again. He got back into the car and tried to start it. Nothing happened, it didn't even turn over. He knew his battery was good but he couldn't understand why it wouldn't start. He pulled out his cell phone and tired to call home, but he didn't have any reception. He tried to call other people also but none of them worked. He couldn't understand it.

Kevin laid his head back against his chair and closed his eyes. He took another deep breath and then he let it all out. He cursed and hit steering wheel. He threw all of his work papers around. He picked up his notebook and threw it at the passenger side window cracking it slightly. He was rambling around and cursing like a wild talking bull that wanted to be let free from his life of slavery. He knew doing all of this wouldn't make it any better and he keep hearing his grandfather's words, "everything has a good side to it." He put his hands over his ears and tried to shut out the words but he couldn't. He opened his car door and rolled out of the car onto the gravel. He then put his head on the ground and screamed until the words of his grandfather had left him. He started to cry for a moment and then he leaned against this car and gasped for air. Once he caught his breath he got back into the car and tried it one last time. It didn't work. Then he got out of the car and just sat there. He didn't know what to do and it seemed foolish of him to have acted like he did and now he was trying to get himself back together. Soon he got to his feet and started to walk. He knew there was a gas station farther up the road and he wondered if they had anything that would help him get his car started. The only problem with that was he didn't know what was wrong with the car other than it wouldn't start. There could be hundreds of things wrong with a car if it wouldn't start and the main reason would be a bad engine. He couldn't believe that. He had just spent almost two thousand dollars getting that engine and if there was something wrong with it he would sue the place or they'd have to fix it for free. He would rather have them fix it so he could just move on, but while he thought about it, he knew it would be better to sue because he would probable end up doing that anyways.

He continued walking down the road thinking to himself that he had to get through this and get home. He looked at his watch to see what time it was and it read twelve. He couldn't believe it. At first he thought it was broken but then he saw the small hand moving around and knew that it was working. All he could conclude from this is that he must have imagined that it was twelve before when it was an earlier time. That made perfect sense, right? So he ignored the time and just kept walking. He had lost a lot of strength from losing his temper and his legs felt heavy as he walked. He had only gotten about two meters away from the car but it felt like miles to his feet. He saw a dead squirrel on the side of the road and he could tell that it had been run over. Someone had moved it over so it could have a peaceful death. The squirrel did three things for Kevin. Number one: he thought he would have been better off dead like the squirrel and he wouldn't have to worry about being stuck out here. He would have to worry about the war that he had run away from like a coward, and then he wouldn't be anxious about what his wife was doing and where she was going all of the time. Number two: it made him hungry. He hadn't eaten since six that evening and would have been okay for the rest of the day if he had made it home on time. He would be sleeping right now and wouldn't have to worry about anything. He would know where his wife was and what his children were doing. He could have already given them the game and he would have been pleased to see their smiles once they got it (well, at least a smile from the youngest of his sons). Number three: it reminded him of his grandfather, but that's a story for later. While he thought of these things he almost missed the house that was to the left of the road. He thought that he could go and at least ask if he could use the phone.

Kevin hesitated a moment and then he started to walk down the gravel road that led to the house. The house was blue in color, but looked black during the night while the moon shined down on it. Tonight the moon was up and Kevin was amazed at how black the house was. There was a shed that was off to the side of the house and Kevin could see a pond behind the house. There were lots of trees along the highway and along the outside of the shed, but none inside of the yard. The gravel road that led up to the house had lots of trash on it. It looked as if a dog or something had come and ripped up the garbage and spread it out around the yard. The house had a garden in front of it but it had a strange kind of arrangement. There was one live and pretty flower followed by a dead and ugly one. This pattern went around the entire outside of the house. The house was also in the shape of a decagon with a cone shaped roof. Kevin had never seen a house like this and he figured that it most have been made especial for the owner. As he got closer to the house it stared to rain and Kevin could hear the great thunderstorm that was coming their way. Right before he knocked he saw lightning coming down from the sky just a few meters away from the yard.

A woman answered the door. She looked as if she was in her twenties and had long beautiful red hair. She was wearing a red robe that matched her hair. Kevin thought she looked weird because she had red hair, a red robe, and green eyes. Her skin was very pale like she didn't get out into the sun much. She was surprised to see anyone out here, especially this late. She didn't even know this man and she was sure he wanted to use the phone or something. What Kevin didn't know about her is that she was insane, and was no longer in control of her own mind half of the time. She had been a widow many times and her last husband's death had paid for her to build this house the way she liked it. She had done it this way because he believed that she had nine other people living inside of her body also. She had kept them at bay for many years now and she was more than willing to give up her insanity and pass on over to the other side.

Kevin just looked at her for a moment and then he spoke.

"Hey, do you think I could use your phone?" he asked as politely as he could.

"Well, I don't know. I don't even know you," she said about to close the door.

"Hey, please! My cell phone won't work and this rain is coming. Just one phone call. Please!"

"Okay, just wait here until I come back." She closed the door and left him out in the rain. She then went to her room and looked inside of the closet. That is where her shotgun was. She had to look around for the bullets and once she found them she looked inside of the case. There was only one bullet left. She put it into the gun and then went back to get Kevin. He had been out in the rain for about five minutes and was starting to walk away when the woman came to the door with her gun. Kevin turned around and was frighten by the sight of the gun.

"What is that for?" asked Kevin, putting his hands out in front of him trying to shield himself.

"This is because I don't trust anyone. I'm going to let you call and then you'll leave this house whether it is still raining or not," she said with the gun shaking in her hands.

"Okay, thank you for your help." Kevin then walked up the steps and into the house. It looked fastidious and everything was neat. Kevin could tell that she had some money because she had expensive pictures all over the walls, expensive vases set up all through the house, and because when Kevin bent over to tie his shoes he felt the carpet and knew it was animal fur. All of the walls on the inside were painted blue, and the carpet extended throughout the entire house. The house had ten rooms inside of it and all of them had the same bed, the same color, the same everything.

"The kitchen is to the left," said the woman. "Please don't touch anything. I just got done cleaning."

"Okay," said Kevin as he walked into the kitchen. "And once again I thank you for you help."

"Ya, whatever," said the woman as she walked back into her room to put on some clothes.

"Hey, will you tell me your name?"

"Yes, it's Rachael." Kevin was now in the kitchen and he picked up the phone. He looked around the clean kitchen and noticed the refrigerator. Just the sight of it made him hungry. He was wondering what she might have had in it, but then he shook his head and dialed the number of his home. The phone started ringing and his oldest son, Keith, picked up the phone and said "hello," but Kevin never heard his son say that because the phone had cut off once he had heard someone had picked up. He hung the phone up and tried to dial again, but he didn't even get a dial tone this time. He angrily hung up the phone and turned to find Rachael looking at him. She was laughing because she figured that the phone line would have been struck down.

"Excuse me, but what is so funny?" asked Kevin with an irate tone.

"I'm sorry, but I thought that was going to happen. I didn't want you to get your hopes down. I guess you should leave now." Kevin just looked at her and then walked past her to the door. He was about to leave when the lights went out. He was going to tell Rachael that he could fix it for her, but she came up behind him and held the gun on his back.

"Are you trying to kill me?" said Rachael in a bloodcurdling voice.

"No, Mama. I don't even know what happen."

"I don't believe you."

"Hey, I'm an electrician. I can try to fix this for you."

"You can?"

"Yes, if you let me."

"All right, I'll take you to the basement." She then took the gun from Kevin's back and led him to the door of the basement.

"Here's the door. Hey, take this flashlight with you. It might be dark down there."

"Thank you," said Kevin as he took the flashlight from the woman and opened the door to the basement. He turned on the flashlight and started walking down the stairs. He turned around to look at see if Rachael was still there and she was. *She must be crazy or something,* thought Kevin as he walked down the stairs. *I should have just waited in the car until tomorrow, but now I'm in the crazy lady's house and she might kill me. After this I'm going to try to stay cool and maybe calm her down.* He heard another thundering sound from outside. *I don't think that I'm going to be able to leave tonight anyways.* Kevin had just reached the bottom of the stairs and Rachael screamed, "Look to the left and you should find the fuse box."

"Okay." Kevin then turned to the left and looked for the fuse box. He was expecting to run into some spider webs or to see some rats, but the basement looked even cleaner than the upstairs. There was a sofa that had plastic over it and a table that was so clean that the light from his flashlight reflected right back at him with even greater force. There was a TV but it wasn't plugged up, and the only boxes were stacked neatly on the other side of the room. He walked along the wall and in the corner of the room he found the fuse box. He tried to open it but it wouldn't move. It looked as if someone had jammed it somehow. Kevin had a screwdriver in his pocket and he used it to open the box. Inside everything looked fine. He couldn't see anything wrong with any of it. While he was looking he heard someone up stairs talking to Rachael. It sounded like an older woman's voice so Kevin thought it was her grandma, and just went back to work. He was checking out the wires that ran throughout the house when the lights came back on.

He looked around and figure that he must have done something to get the light to come on; he just didn't know what. He walked back up to meet Rachael still standing by the door.

"Thank you for turning the lights back on," said Rachael as she reach forward and hugged him.

"You're welcome, but you helped me first, remember?" He felt uncomfortable hugging her but he didn't want to get on her bad side.

"I'm going to get you something good to eat. I'm sure you must be hungry. You poor thing, I'm so sorry. Having to be in that rain and all that. I'm sorry that I made you stand out there like that. I should have known you couldn't have been all that bad."

"Well, thank you, Rachael. I would really appreciate some food." He followed her back to the kitchen. He was glad that she was no longer carrying the gun around with her. He now felt a lot safer around her. They got to the kitchen and she told him to sit down at the table. She had ordered some pizza only an hour before Kevin had shown up; it was still hot so she put some on a plate and brought it to him.

"There I hope you'll like it. It's pepperoni. Everyone likes that, right?"

"Thank you," said Kevin as he stuffed his mouth.

"Wait. I'll get you a drink." Rachael then got up and fixed Kevin something to drink. Then she just sat there and stared at him as he ate. Once he was finish she wanted to get to know him. This had been the first moment in months that she had had full control over her body and she wanted to make the best out of it.

"So why did you come here?"

"Oh, my car broke down. I couldn't use my phone for some reason. It wouldn't work. So I got out and started walking, and then I saw your house and thought you might help me."

"I guess you thought right. Do you live around here?"

"No, I live a long ways down the road. I was hoping to make it home some time tonight, but it seems as if I won't be going anywhere tonight."

"So you have a family?"

"Yes, I have three sons. I try to raise them right but sometimes they just get out of hand…" he continued talking, trying to clam his nerves. He still didn't feel that comfortable around her and he didn't want her to get upset or anything. Rachael, on the other hand, was having a good time talking to Kevin. She hoped that he would be the first person in two years that she could talk to and not kill. She didn't feel the others anywhere, but she didn't know that they were just hiding.

36

"So do you have a wife?" she asked, smiling.

"Yes. I've been married now for twenty-five years. What about you?"

"I've been divorced now for twenty-five years. Well, that was my first one. I've had about five husbands. I really don't count the ones after the first one, because we weren't really in love."

That shocked Kevin. *She must have been insane and killed most of her other husbands for the money,* thought Kevin. He now knew that he had to play it cool and be as nice as possible to make it out of here safe. It was going to be hard, but it had to be done.

"I can't believe that you are that old. You look about eighteen. How do you do it?"

Rachel smiled and then said boldly, "I just stopped aging one day."

"Ya," Kevin laughed out loud. "And how did you do that?"

"I don't know I just..." Then she paused. Her face started to shake it looked as if she was about to have a seizure. She put her hands over her ears and started to scream. Kevin reached over the table and tried to help her, but she moved and fell off of the chair. Kevin stood up and looked down at her and he saw a different person. Rachael was now an old woman. They looked nothing alike to Kevin. It wasn't like she just turned old, but she had turned into a different person. Kevin stood still in shock as the woman got up. Her eyes were as black as the night sky and they sent a chill down Kevin's back. He was about to run when the woman pulled out a knife from her clothes and stabbed Kevin's hand into the table. It happened very quickly and Kevin didn't even see it coming. Kevin reached down and pulled the knife out of his hand. The blood had gotten everywhere and Kevin was shaking with fright. He wasn't afraid of the wound, because he had been to war and seen worse things than a cut hand. He was frightened because of Rachael and her transformation. He didn't believe in such things and didn't want to. He had seen it with his own eyes but would still walk out of this house and tell everyone he knew that Rachael was just insane and that she had done it. He would never tell a soul that her body had changed into an older woman and then stabbed him. That truth would never reach his lips.

He tried to stab the old woman with the knife but she caught his hand before he could hit her. She then twisted it and made him drop the knife. As it fell towards the ground the old woman moved her other hand and with great speed caught the knife before it hit. She then held the knife up and smiled at Kevin. It was an evil smile, and Kevin had never seen anything that malevolent. He just stood there trying to think of what he could do. There weren't too many options because he knew that she was too fast for him to try to hit her. He thought maybe she couldn't run that fast. She was only an old woman. He moved slowly to the side of the table and tried to run, but before he could reach the door the old woman appeared and blocked his way. He didn't see her at first and he ran straight into her. She didn't move back or even feel him hitting her. It was as if she couldn't feel pain. Kevin, on the other hand, went falling back and he felt like he had run into a brick wall. He shook his head, and got to his feet, and looked to see what he had run into. He was sure that he hadn't hit the wall. He looked up to find the woman right in the middle of the doorway leading out of the kitchen. All she did was smile. After this Kevin was sure that she was either a robot or something else, but not human.

"Rachael, why are you doing this? What are you?" asked Kevin, moving his way slowly into the other part of the kitchen.

"Rachael?" said the old woman. "That slut isn't worth anything. All she does is complain and fuss, I've been waiting to get rid of her. But you I like. You should be next."

"What...what happened to Rachael?"

"She's here, don't you see her. Look!" The old woman pointed to the floor underneath the table. Rachael was there. She was gagged and tied up. She was squirming trying to get free, but the knots were too tight. She had a deep cut in her head and blood was leaking out from it. Kevin moved towards her but the woman stopped him. She put the knife up against his neck and backed him up.

"Let her be. Soon she'll be free. She wasn't being cooperative, but soon she'll learn. She wanted it all for herself. I wouldn't let her! But you, you can have it all. You're the one we all have been waiting for to carry our soul. You should be able to control it. Let's just hope you don't go insane."

"What do you mean?"

"Don't you see?" The old woman backed up from Kevin and then she started to wave her hands around the room and turn in a circle. Then more people started to appear. There was a black man of about forty. He had bruises all around his body. He didn't have a shirt on and on the left side of his chest there was a deep wound. He was bleeding from the wound and it was dripping down his body and on to the ground. His eyes were gone and there blood coming from his sockets. It looked like he had been in some kind of fight or something and had been cut up with claws. Next, a little girl appeared. She was holding a teddy bear that was missing a head and it had lots of blood on it. Her hair had blood in it and all of it on the right side was missing showing Kevin all of the cuts that were on her scalp. She looked like she was about five years old, but she had makeup on her face that could mean she was a lot older than she looked. She opened her mouth and most of her teeth were missing, but the teeth that were still there weren't small enough to be baby teeth. All in all she looked like a mess and it seemed to Kevin that she must have died a horrible death. After her came three more men. They were all Mexican, and looked as if they were triplets. Also they had on straw hats that were as identical as their faces. They looked at Kevin and then took off their hat to reveal that they no longer had a forehead or anything else that was supposed to be above their eyebrows. It looked as if something had just sliced the top part of their heads off. Though, they no longer had a brain, they were still smiling. In fact they were the only ones out of all of the people that came that had a smile on their faces. Soon after them came another man. He had a cross across his chest about twelve inches long and the inside of the cross was gone and you could see through the hole and to the other side of the man. He had many tattoos across his body and he was bald. One of his tattoos read, "What would Jesus do?" He had on church pants and shoes that were very clean. It was as if he was on his way to church that very minute. After him came another old woman. This one was crying with her hands on her face. She looked a lot older than the other woman and she had all gray hair. Her face was very wrinkled and looked as if it might fall off at any minute.

Her hand was bleeding. It was covered in blood and in the middle of it there were bite marks. It looked like a human bite not one done by an animal or anything. She had on a dress that was covered in blood, but there weren't any other cuts on her so it couldn't have been her own. Then came the last of them. It was a boy of about four feet tall. He looked just like a child, but his skin was of a grayish color. He smiled at Kevin and showed him his teeth that were full of blood. This child was the only one of the things that had no wounds or bruises. All there was on him was as black dot that looked like it was about the size of a bullet on his forehead.

The old woman had been turning around with her hand up this whole time and once they were all out she stopped and looked at Kevin. She then changed. She had changed into nurse's clothes instead of just a nightgown like she had had on before.

"I hope we'll learn to like each other," she said as she and the rest of the people walked forward towards Kevin. He walked backwards as far as he could and then fell to the ground and put his hands over her eyes and started to scream. He did this and thought of his grandfather. He thought of the words he had always told him and of how he wished that he was here with him now. He grandfather had done a lot for him and he wished he'd had the chance to thank him. After this he opened his eyes and saw that everyone was gone. He crawled over to the table to see if Rachael was there but she was also gone. He then got up and went to the sink to wash out his wound, but it wasn't there anymore. He thought that he must have been dreaming and that he had lost his mind, but then how would he have gotten into this house. He had never been here before and never wished to come back. He looked at the table and saw that the pizza was still there. So Rachael must have been here at one time and he couldn't have been that crazy, as to imagine someone giving him some food. *She must be here somewhere,* thought Kevin as he started to search the house. He looked everywhere and found nothing until he looked in her bedroom. She was lying there with blood on her head just like when she was under the table. There was a note on her body, but Kevin didn't touch it or her. Once he saw the body he just turned around and ran out of the room.

It was still raining outside but Kevin couldn't stay inside of the house with a dead body. He wasn't afraid of her or anything, but he didn't want to be framed for her death. He didn't know how she had died, but he knew that it had something to do with the old lady. The storm had gotten much worse and he almost couldn't run because the wind was so strong it dragged him in the direction it was blowing. Soon he got to the end of the driveway and he was glad that the wind was blowing in the direction of his car. He ran all the way over to it and quickly jumped in. He had forgotten that it didn't work and he tried to start it. Soon it began to run and then he remembered. He thought maybe he should have just stayed with his car and just tried it until it started; he wished he had stayed in his car. He quickly put it in drive and drove on down the road. He looked at his watch to see what time it was; it read 12:01. In all that time only a minute had gone by. He couldn't believe that. He was positive that the watch was broken and he took it off and threw it out the window.

He was no longer sleepy and he wasn't going to stop for anything. If his car had broken down again he would have walked the rest of the way home. Nothing was going to stop him from getting off of this road and out of this storm. He didn't ever want to drive down this road again. The first thing he would do after he got some sleep was to change his route, even if it took him longer to get to work and to get home. He didn't care about the gas, because his company would pay for that; he would just be out a little later.

He wasn't sure if he should go to the police and tell them what had happened (he had made up a story about her being dead when he got there and all he did was look and leave. He wasn't going to tell them about what really happened, because he wasn't sure if it had really happened. All he knew was that someone had killed Rachael and he knew it wasn't him.) Or if he should just leave it alone and act like he had never been there. He hoped that she had killed herself and left a suicide letter and then he would have nothing to worry about. But what if it wasn't? What if the old woman had really been there and she was trying to frame him? Now he wished he had read the letter.

He continued driving down the road and soon he came to the cross with the snake. He looked straight at it as he drove and didn't pay any attention to anything else. He wondered if that grave and the boy who was supposed to have died there, the same boy he had seen before. The man that had told him the story had never said anything about the child having gray skin. If that were true then the people would have killed him long before they had. How could his skin have turned gray? It was just impossible for him to have lived with gray skin and have lived among the rest of the people. They would have thought he was a warlock or a demon. Kevin thought that maybe all of them were victims of that child and he still had control over them, but then why did the old lady seem to have control of everything. It was all a mystery to him.

He had been thinking all of this and not watching the road. There was someone off in the distance and they were waiting for him to drive up. He then realized that he was still driving and tried to watch where he was going. He couldn't see the road all that well, but he thought he had seen someone. He slowed down some to see if they would move out of the way or finish walking across the road, but they didn't move. He didn't stop. Just kept driving, because he thought it was just a shadow and soon it was gone, so he figured he was right. After a while he came to another shadow of a person. This one looked even more like a shadow than the other one and he was sure that it was a shadow. He continued to drive and soon he hit something. The front of his car was dented from this object and it looked as if he had run into a pole about five feet wide. He hadn't put on a seat belt and he went crashing into the windshield of his car.

He hit his head against the windshield, but he didn't go crashing through it. There was a huge crack and a piece of glass was in Kevin's forehead. He pushed away from the front of the car so he could get his head off the windshield. He then took out the piece of glass that was in his head and threw it into the passenger seat. He screamed from the pain and then he got out of the car. It was raining harder now and he couldn't see anything because of it. He had hit his ribs against the steering wheel and it had knocked the breath out of him and broken one of his ribs. He tried to walk but it was hard to just stand up right let alone walk. He moved over to the side of the road and tried to walk in the direction of his home. He could see someone in front of him, but he didn't know whom. Soon he was close enough to see and he was shocked to find the same old woman from the house standing before him.

She walked up to him and knocked him down. Then she smiled in his face.

"I can't believe that you tried to run me over. Didn't you see me?"

"What are…are…you talking about?"

"Well, we'll see each other soon enough." Then she hit him on the forehead and knocked him unconscious.

Kevin didn't wake up until the next day. He found himself in a hospital lying inside of a bed. He had a broken arm and a fracture to his skull. He had an IV running to his arm and he couldn't move because he was still moderately drugged. He was also still in a lot of pain. It wasn't just any kind of pain neither. He couldn't understand why he felt this way. He knew that it was pain, but it also reminded him of joy and happiness. It was just too weird of a feeling for Kevin to even explain it so when the nurse asked him how he felt he just said "okay" and left it at that.

It took them awhile to get in, but when they did Kevin was pleased to be surrounded by his family. His children looked glad to see him and even his wife looked concerned. He had thought that she wouldn't even show up, but he was happily mistaken. All of his kids came around him and they were all talking about what had happened to him, but he was too drowsy to understand them. He fell asleep after a while and they had to wait for him to wake up before he could hear what had happened. They told him that he had sat out in the rain the night before for about three hours. Then someone came driving down the road and almost ran into his car. They got out and found Kevin knocked out. He quickly called the police and an ambulance. About three hours later Kevin's family found out about what happened. His wife was just getting home from the church and she didn't want to drive all the way over to the hospital to just wait until they let them in to see Kevin. So they waited a few hours and then they drove over to the hospital. Once they got there they sat in the room for about two hours until Kevin woke up. Once he retained all of this he started to feel pain again. This time it was real pain and he started to scream. His wife ran out of the room and got the nurse and soon Kevin was drugged again and taken to surgery to be operated on.

At first Kevin just opened one of his eyes and then he started to move. Everyone in the room quickly moved over to his side and waited for him to speak. He looked at everyone, but he was too drugged to see their faces and they were just blobs of nothing to him. His wife was getting tired of waiting to see if he was okay so she left the boys and went out to get them some lunch. Soon after she left, the drugs wore off and Kevin woke up. He was surprised to see his sons waiting there for him.

"Hey, what are all of you doing?" asked Kevin, looking around the room at all three of his sons. Keith was the only one that was still awake and he went over to William, the second oldest, and woke him up and then to James, the youngest. Then they all walked over to their father and hugged him.

"How long have I been in here?" asked Kevin.

"Well," said William. "It's five now and they found you about 5:03 this morning, so I'd say about twelve hours and three minutes."

"You always have to be so exact about everything," said Keith. "You could have just said twelve hours and gotten the same effect."

"Well, one of us has to be the smart one."

"You mean the nerd!"

"Hey, stop fussing," said Kevin. "Can you see I'm in pain and you two and sitting there fussing? You should be happy that I'm still here. Hey where is your mother?"

"She left to go and get us some lunch," said James.

"Why did she wait this long to go and get lunch?"

"She wanted to make sure that you were okay, I guess?" said Keith. Kevin hoped that was true, and maybe his marriage could last. It could have just as easily have been a lie and she could have just gone to find something else to do other than sit in here with him. He would just have to wait and see.

"So what have all of you been doing all of this time?"

"We just sat in here waiting for you to wake up," said Keith. "I didn't want you to die and I not have been here with you. I would have hated myself for the rest of my life."

"Yes, Father. Head injures are very hard to be operated on and you could have easily died," said William.

"They operated on my head?"

"No, Father, the wound wasn't deep enough to need operation I was just saying that if it did it wouldn't have been an easy task to complete. There could have been lots of difficulties and many things could have gone wrong..."

"I think we get the point," said Keith, waiting for William to shut up.

"It's all right, Keith, I'm just glad to hear your voices. I'm so glad that I'm here with all of you today."

"Hey, Dad. You don't have to get all sensitive and all that. We love you to." They continued talking and Kevin was overjoyed that he was still alive. He couldn't imagine what would have happened if he had died last night. Then the images of last night came to him. He was starting to remember the old woman and everything. He had hoped that it was only a dream and he had been sleep driving or something, but he couldn't ignore all of the facts that proved what happened was true. While he was thinking over his facial expression had turned blank and his children were frightened that something was wrong with him.

"Dad, what's wrong? Are you okay?" asked Keith as he shook his father trying to snap him out of his trance. "William, go and get the doctor and tell him that Dad woke up but now something's wrong with him."

"Okay." Then William quickly got up and walked out of the room. James had started to cry and scream out "Daddy" hoping that he would somehow wake up.

"Stop that," said Keith. "Crying never helps anything. I know I've told you that before." Then James stopped crying and he walked over to a chair, sat down, and closed his eyes. Keith continued to shake his father until he woke up. Kevin had no idea that he had blacked out like that and he was frightened when Keith told him he had done so.

"Where did William go?"

"He went to get the doctor. Just lie down, Dad. It'll be okay. Just stay calm." Keith continued to say all of these things until the doctor and William came into the room. It was Doctor Smith. He had been Kevin's doctor since he was a little child. He had treated Kevin when he had the chicken pox and up until he was a teenager. That was when Kevin found out what he had done. The doctor was a family doctor so also treated the rest of his family. One day his mother had gone to him to talk about her husband and soon they started an affair. It lasted for about a year, before Kevin's father found out. That was the last straw and the last thing that made him go insane. When Kevin found out about this he told the doctor that he would never come back to this hospital and that he would never forgive him. But now looking at him he was almost happy that he had treated him, because Kevin was always told that there was nothing Doctor Smith couldn't cure.

The doctor had a familiar smile on his face and he walked up to Kevin and greeted him nicely.

"So how have you been all these years?" asked the doctor. He looked a lot older and fatter than Kevin remembered him, but it had been about twenty years since he had seen him.

"I'm good," said Kevin weakly. Even though he was happy to see him he could not stand the thought of having to speak with him.

"You have wonderful children. This one seems very intelligent," he said, putting his hand on William. William just smiled with satisfaction. "He told me that he thought you were suffering from some kind of coma. How do you feel?"

"I'm fine. It's just I got a flashback of what happened last night."

"Well, would you tell us what happened, then?"

"I don't remember everything," said Kevin. He was lying. He didn't want them to know the truth about everything. He wouldn't tell them about the old woman or about all of the people he had seen. One reason was because he didn't want to worry his children and the other because even though he and the doctor knew each other he would never believe a story like this one. So he quickly tired to make up a lie and was relieved when his wife walked in. She had bought the children

Burger King and she almost dropped it when she saw that Kevin was awake. She then walked over to the chair that James was sitting in and laid the food in front of him. Once she was done with that she walked over to Kevin's bed.

"I'm happy to see you, Samantha," said Kevin, looking at her.

"I'm glad to see you to," said Samantha as she started to cry, but soon she sucked it back in. She threw her arms around him. She held him for about thirty seconds and then finally let him go. As she was letting him go Kevin looked at her face. He was shocked. He felt the skin on his face grow cold. Everything froze. She looked just like Rachael. Her hair was still black, but her face looked just like Rachael's. It only lasted for a moment, but Kevin jumped back from Samantha with a frightening look on his face.

"What's wrong?" asked Samantha.

"Yes, you look like something is hurting you. Are you alright?" asked Doctor Smith, walking closer to Kevin. Kevin just stood still and looked at both of them in shock and then he spoke.

"Yes, I'm...fine. You must have touched a soft spot on my back. There was a sharp pain that went down my spine, but I'm fine now."

"Are you sure?" asked the doctor, reaching over to Kevin.

"Yes, yes. I'm fine." They were all silent for a moment and then Samantha spoke.

"I was so worried about you, Kevin. I was at home waiting for you to get in and when you didn't come I went over to the church to pray with Father Lindo. He and I prayed all night and then I came home to find out that you had been in some kind of car wreck. I came as fast as I could and I thought you might not ever wake up. Now I'm so glad that you're awake. I don't know what I would have done." Then she started to cry again. Kevin reached out his hand and put it on her shoulder. Then he turned his head towards Keith.

"Take your brothers to the cafeteria and eat your lunch."

"Alright, Dad." Then Keith got William and went over to get James. He didn't want to go but went once Kevin told him so they all left together. Once he was sure they were gone he started to tell them his story. Or you could say his lie.

"I got caught up in a traffic jam and I got to my store late. I didn't feel like working but I had to because I wanted to get it out of the way. So I when in and it took me about two or three hours to get done with that store and then I went to get back on the road. I was hungry so I went to go get something to eat. There weren't that many stores that were open so I had to go to Taco Bell and that was all the way on the other side of town. So I went there and then came back to get on the road. By then it was…" He stopped talking and looked up at the ceiling. He couldn't help remembering that he had seen twelve o'clock on his watch the entire night.

"What's wrong?" asked Samantha. "Are you—"

But Kevin cut her off. "No, I'm fine. By that time it was around one o'clock. I was tired of driving and stopped at a shop to get something to keep me awake. I wanted some coffee, but their machine was broken and I had to get a Doctor Pepper instead. Then I got back on the road and continued to drive. Soon I got down the road to where that cr…" He stopped for a moment, but then he continued.

"Then I got to the part of the road where the cross was and saw something in the road in front of me. Something was out there but I couldn't see what it was. I slowed down but it didn't move and I thought it was just a shadow. It was and I just drove past it and soon I came to another one. I thought this one was a shadow too but then I ran into something and hit the windshield. I then got up and out of the car and tired to walk away, but soon I fainted and fell down on the side of the road."

"Did you get a chance to see what hit you?" asked Doctor Smith. Kevin was silent for a moment and then he shook his head "no." When Doctor Smith had asked him that question he had seen a flashback of the old lady and almost threw up.

"Well, they showed your car on the news and it looked as if you hit a moose or something. I say that you're lucky to still be alive."

"How long will he be in here, Doctor?" asked Samantha, moving closer to Kevin.

"He should be able to leave by tomorrow and I'll have to get him some painkillers. Kevin, you shouldn't have any more problems, and we checked your head for tumors and didn't find anything. I suggest that you come back in a week and then I'll see how you're doing then."

"Thank you, Doctor," said Kevin. "I'm so glad to see you again."

"And the same to you both." And with that the doctor left the two of them alone. Soon Samantha walked up beside him and got into his bed. She did it softly because she didn't want to cause him any more pain. Then she started to rub his stomach and she put her leg across his body. Soon she was kissing Kevin. Kevin had just sat there and enjoyed the moment. It had been a long time since they had had a moment together like this and Kevin didn't want anything to ruin it. They had been silent all of this time, but after a while Kevin broke the silence.

"I love you, Samantha."

"I love you too," said Samantha as she leaned over to kiss him. "Do you want us to stay here with you?"

"No, I think I'll be alright, and I'm sure that Keith had some kind of party or something to go to. And I know the police will come to see me about the wreck soon and I'll tell them the story. I don't want you to have to stay here on my account. Go and have a good day."

"Okay, I'll go and get the kids and we'll see you tomorrow." She kissed him one last time and then left the room. Soon Kevin fell asleep and he had a dream about her. He hoped that he could take the opportunity to turn his life around and get closer to his wife. Even though he didn't believe in God any longer, he was even willing to do that just to stay close to his wife. He would do anything for her for the time being and he planned to keep it that way. He would have gone to hell and back just to have her say that she loved him again. There was nothing that could have stopped him from doing whatever she desired. There was nothing that was going to get in the way of his love.

The police came later on that day to get his statement about what had happened and he told Doctor Smith to tell them that he had to rest and they would have to come back again tomorrow. He was starting to like him all over again. He was the closest thing to a father (other than his grandfather) that he had ever had. He used to come and talk to him about everything he couldn't tell anyone else. Doctor Smith was the person that had given him his first cigarette and his first beer. He had taken Kevin to all of the parties that no one else would give him a ride to and when he ran away from home he could go straight to his house. Kevin could almost not believe that he had let one thing he had done wrong split them apart. All people make mistakes, right, and Kevin certainly didn't think of himself as being any better than he was. The more Kevin thought about it the more he knew that he would have to give the doctor another chance. Hopefully things would be better.

Kevin soon got restless sitting in that bed and he got up to walk around the hospital. Visiting hours were over and not many people were walking around. Soon he came to a window and looked out to watch the sunset. There's not one person in the entire world that doesn't think the sunset isn't beautiful. It always reminded Kevin of his wife and her beauty. He had asked her to marry him one day when they were on the beach. He hoped that he would get the chance to take his whole family to that beach one day. It was in Texas, but every time they got the chance to go something else came up and they had to try again next year. This year Kevin was determined to get them down there even if he had to quit his job and sell everything he owned. If it came down to that Kevin could always get a job down there as a lifeguard or something. That was the only time Kevin ever thought that the army helped him in any way.

Kevin stood there until the sunset could no longer be seen. He started to walk away when he noticed something in the corner of his eye. This figure was up against the window and Kevin could feel something telling him to look. After he did he wished he had not. It was the old lady that Kevin had seen the day before. She still had a smile on her face and looked twice as malevolent as before. She was nude and there was blood everywhere on her body. It was just the most malicious thing Kevin had ever seen and he quickly tried to shut his eyes, but they were frozen on her body as if she was the girl of his dreams or something of great beauty. It seemed as if every second Kevin looked at her she got more spiteful and vicious. Soon Kevin got his senses back and he jumped back into someone who was walking by. They both hit the wall and then fell to the ground. The person got to his feet first and he promptly helped Kevin to his feet. It was Doctor Smith.

"What are you doing out here? Are you okay?" asked the doctor, looking very concerned. He still had feelings for Kevin even though he hadn't seen him for years. He didn't want anything to happen to him and still thought of him as his own child. He would have given anything to go back to the day that he had told him about his mother and himself and taken it all back. That way they wouldn't have gone astray all those years and now they would still have been friends.

"Yes, I'm fine," said Kevin as he got to his feet.

"What did you jump into me for? Did you see something through the window? Did something frighten you?" The doctor said this looking Kevin straight in the eyes.

"No, I was just tripping," said Kevin, shaking his head.

"Well, I can see that and you made me trip also." Then they both laughed and Doctor Smith walked with Kevin back to his room.

"So what line of work are you into nowadays?" asked the doctor with his hand on Kevin's back.

"I'm an electrician, now."

"What did you do before that?"

"I was in the army."

"Ya, I heard about all that war stuff, but I don't have much time to watch TV." He took out a cigarette and lit it. He offered Kevin one but he declined. "I got a chance to watch that tape about the man that was decapitated and I couldn't believe that."

"Maybe that wouldn't have happened if I would have stayed in the army," said Kevin, remembering the man.

"No, I think you did the right thing. It's a lost cause over there and they'll end up gaining much of nothing. I'm not that religious but I know that people will cause their own end. It's just a matter of time until it happens. It all seems sad, don't you think so?"

"Well, I'd say that they deserve it. With all of the bad things that people do. I think that it best for humans to destroy themselves that way it will be their own fault in the end."

"You're so cruel. You shouldn't let all of the bad things that happened to you change the way you look at other people. Not everyone is as bad as me and your father."

"Ya, but most of them are." By this time they were in front of Kevin's room and he went in and closed the door behind him without saying goodbye. He still had feelings for the doctor also, but he wanted nothing to do with him. After he got out of this hospital he hoped that he would never have to look him in the face every again and then he could use the rest of his life to try to forget him. If it took that long.

He had trouble sleeping that night. He didn't dream of the night before or anything; in fact, he didn't dream at all. He couldn't get to sleep. He felt his body changing the entire night. It went from hot to cold, and then from cold to hot. He felt like something was ripping him inside and out. He screamed one time and the nurse come to check on him. He told her that he was fine and that she should leave him alone. The pain only got worse as he sat in the bed so he took some of the painkillers that the doctor had left him. Instead of killing the pain they seemed to feed it. He didn't know where the pain was coming from. He had taken classes on human anatomy and he knew how all of the blood vessels transmitted pain. This pain just felt like it was coming from his skin. Like someone had taken his skin off like it was a coat or something and put it in the drier to heat it up. He went through this pain for most of the night and then it just disappeared. He didn't know what stopped it, because he stopped taking the painkillers hours ago. Now his body felt peaceful and tranquil. It was almost as if he was fully healed. His head no longer hurt and his arm felt like it was brand-new. He didn't know what did it but he made up his mind to thank Doctor Smith for whatever he had done to rid him of his pain. Now he almost hoped that one day Doctor Smith and he could become friends like they had been before. Then it occurred to Kevin that if he had never been with his mother then they would have never been friends. Was it worth having his father go insane to have Doctor Smith? Kevin would never know because he really didn't remember his father or even stabbing him in the back. The only reason he knew he had done that was because one of the policemen hadn't died yet and told the police before he did. The only thing Kevin remembered about his father was that he had brought him a BB gun. He took Kevin outside and showed him how to use it. He sited it at a bird and shot it out of the tree. Kevin hated his father for doing that, and he picked the bird up off of the ground. He tired to help it and he prayed to God to bring it back to life, but nothing ever happened. His father laughed at him and told him that if there were a God he would never have brought him into this world. About a day later Mark left and Kevin didn't see him again for four years.

Soon the sun rose and Kevin got out of his bed to go to the bathroom. Even though the pain had left him during the night he still couldn't get to sleep and now he was exhausted. He almost couldn't stand up to walk to the bathroom. He hadn't taken a bath in two days and his own smell was starting to get to him. He couldn't believe that he had let himself smell like that and the doctor and his family hadn't said anything to him. They just let him walk around like everything was fine. After he got done in the bathroom, he sat back on his bed and tried to go back to sleep. About an hour later Doctor Smith came in to check on him. The doctor saw that he was sleeping and tried to sit down quietly, but he woke Kevin up as he sat down.

"Hey, you don't mind if I smoke, do you?" asked Doctor Smith about to light up a cigarette.

"No. Not at all, go ahead," said Kevin as he sat up on the side of the bed.

"It looks like you feel a lot better today. I'm on my break but I had to come and see if you were okay. I'm really sorry for any pain I might have caused you. Can you ever forgive me?" said the doctor, looking ever serious.

Kevin did not say anything for a moment. Then he said, "It's okay. I can't blame you for getting with my mother. It's not like you raped her or anything. She wanted you just as much as you wanted her, right?"

"That's what she always told me. I miss her a lot," said the doctor, smiling inside of himself.

"Me too. At least you didn't have to watch her die," said Kevin, putting his head down.

"It okay, Kevin," said the doctor, putting his hand on Kevin's shoulder. "I know she's in a better place now. I would be happy to get the chance to go and join her. I just hope I can live my life half as well as she did. You know she really didn't want to start an affair. She just wanted someone to talk to. She told me that Mark wouldn't come home at night anymore and that he didn't want to be around her. I told her that she was too pretty to have to worry about a man treating her wrong. She reached out to me and we kissed. Then we just met each other and talked. The day your father found out, we went out to eat at a restaurant and I guess he followed us. I had tried to reason with him before that day even came around but he didn't want me to tell him how to treat his wife. So I'd say that it was his own fault that she left him for me."

"What did you two do after that?"

"Well, we continued to see each other and I moved in with the both of you. Don't you remember that?"

"No, I don't."

"Well, I was there and I hate myself for leaving on your birthday. There was an urgent surgery procurer that I had to do, because the patient wouldn't have anyone else but me. I didn't get home until after all of it happened. I wish that I'd have stayed. The patient ended up dying anyways and there wasn't much that I could have done in the first place."

"No, I glad you weren't there. He may have killed you also. Then I would have no one to talk to right now."

"Ya, maybe it was meant for them to die and not me."

"You mean fate?"

"Ya, fate."

"I'm sorry, but I gave up anything to do with faith a long time ago."

"What do you—" They were interrupted by Kevin's family that just had walked into the room. James ran over to his father and hugged him and the rest of them walked around his bed.

"Hey, Daddy," said James.

"Hey, James," said Kevin, rubbing his son's head.

"Well, I guess you're good to go," said the doctor, getting up. "I'll see you in a week."

"Yes, I'll see you then," said Kevin. Then the doctor left the room.

"Come on, Dad, I'll help you up," said Keith as he pulled his father up to his feet.

"Thank you, son. How are you, William?"

"I'm well, Father. I am just a little worried about you."

"There's no need for you to worry about me," said Kevin as his sons helped him to the door where Samantha was standing. She just looked at them and once they were by the door she grabbed Kevin.

"You just don't know how worried I was about you. I couldn't sleep all night. I just..." Then Kevin kissed her on the lips. They kissed for about fifteen seconds and Keith took his brothers with him to the car.

"I didn't sleep either. I keep thinking of you and the kids. I want things to change. You never know how much time you have left and I don't want to waste another minute," said Kevin as he kissed her again.

"Yes, that's why you should start going to church again. I'm worried about how you're going to end up," she said, pointing her finger towards the ground.

"I'll be fine. You know I don't believe in that stuff anymore." He started walking out of the room and down the hallway.

"But this is a sign. Please come to church with me this evening." Samantha ran up to him and hugged him from behind. Kevin really did not want to give in, but he knew that if he really wanted it to work he had no choice.

"Okay, I'll come for you and only because of you. Not because I'm trying to get back with God, but only because I want to be with you."

"That would make me very happy. I'm so glad to hear that from you. You know that you sat out there for about three hours. You could have died or been eaten by some animals or something."

"Calm down. I'm fine." They continued talking about the day before until they got to their car. Their children were inside, but there were two men standing outside of it. At the time Kevin wasn't really thinking and he thought that something could have been very wrong. He almost went crazy for a moment and was about to grab one of the men by their shirt and pick them off of the ground until he came back to reality. Either way he would have been too weak at the moment to have even moved the man let alone picked him up.

"What's the matter?" asked Kevin.

"Are you Kevin Scott?" said one of the men.

"Yes, that's me. What do you want with me?"

"I'm Detective Roy," said the man on the left as he flashed his badge. "And this is Detective Lance. We need to speak with you."

"Yes, okay." Kevin was relieved that it was the police. "What do you need to know?"

"We need to speak with you about the other day. Do you have a minute?"

"Yes, I—"

He was interrupted by Samantha. "We're on our way home. Will you follow us?" asked Samantha.

"Yes, we'll be right behind you," said Detective Roy, pointing for them to lead the way.

Then they left Kevin and Samantha as they were getting in their car.

"What was that about?" asked Kevin.

"Nothing, I just want to get you home as quickly as possible. I don't want anything else to happen to you," said Samantha as she leaned over and kissed him.

"You need to calm down. I don't think anything else it going to happen to me."

Then they all got into their cars and drove home. They lived about three miles south from the hospital and it took them about fifteen minutes to get home. They lived in a small town called Valleytown. There weren't any other black people that lived in this town, but the Scotts. It's not that Kevin didn't like his own kind or anything, he just got a good deal on the house and he thought it would be a nice place to live. He had never thought about what kind of people lived in that town, and he wasn't racist so it didn't matter to him. The house that he used to live in with his father was around where most of the other black people lived, and that was a place he couldn't live at. His grandparents had raised him in this town but his grandmother died and then his grandfather disappeared. The police looked into his disappearance as some kind of racist killing or something, but they never found any evidence to prove that. So Kevin just moved into their house and now it was paid off and he owned it for the rest of his life. That saved him a lot of the money that he would have spent on a house somewhere else.

The house was the only red brick house on the road. It was the tenth one down the road, and always had a clean-cut yard. The shutters on the house were also red and Kevin had painted them himself. They owned four cars and two of them were in the front. One was for Keith when he got his driver's license and the other was Kevin's car that he had gotten for free from one of his friends before he had left Germany. The house was only one story but had had only four rooms until Kevin had another one added on. Kevin's boat was almost always in the yard. He didn't have much time to go fishing but when he could he would enter one of the fishing contests, though he never won. He just liked the peacefulness of fishing, and winning didn't really matter to him. There was only one thing that bothered Kevin about his abode. It wasn't the white people, because they were just as nice to him as anybody else, but it was the rain. Whenever it would rain their yard would flood. It had flooded when his grandparents had owned it and it was still flooding now. Kevin tried to raise the ground, by putting down some dirt and replanting the grass, but it still flooded. He figured that no matter what he did it would continue to flood and that was the way it was meant to be.

They pulled up into the driveway with the detectives behind them. Kevin got out and walked back to the detectives.

"Follow me. I'll take you to my office," said Kevin as he walked away from the detectives and into the house. It was a little messy. Usually Samantha would make sure that the house was always clean before company came over, but she didn't know that people were coming and didn't have time to clean it. Once they were all inside, the boys went off into their rooms and Kevin could hear Keith yelling at James to leave him alone because he was trying to talk on the phone and didn't have time to play with him. William was in the living room reading a book and Samantha was in the kitchen. Everything seemed just like it had before to Kevin. He felt happy to have made it back to the family that he would do anything for.

"If you want anything to eat, I'm making fried chicken," said Samantha with a huge smile on her face.

"Ya, bring us some into my office," said Kevin as he slid the door open that led to his headquarters.

"Thank you, Mama," said both of the detectives as they walked into Kevin's office. It was on the back of the house. It had once been a back porch, but Kevin turned it into an office so he could work in peace and not have to worry about being bothered. There were two chairs and a desk. Kevin asked the detectives to sit in the chairs. He walked over to the other side of the desk and sat down. Everything on his desk looked just like he had left it. A mess.

"So what do you need to know?" asked Kevin, leaning back in his chair.

"We would like you to tell us everything that happened that day," said Detective Roy. Kevin then told the detective everything he had told his wife and Doctor Smith at the hospital. He had made sure that he memorized that story because he was sure that the police would ask around.

"So you didn't go to anywhere else or anything."

"No, I didn't go anywhere else. Why?"

The detectives turned and looked at each other and then Roy spoke.

"We found a woman dead about a mile down the street."

"Do you think I did it?" asked Kevin calmly.

"Well, you have to be considered as a suspect, but maybe who ever did this to you killed her, and we would want to know why."

"I don't know anyone that lives around there. Why do you think that someone tried to kill me?"

"Well, we found that the thing you hit had the shape of a woman. It couldn't have been anything else and—"

"Well, what else?"

"This is supposed to be a secret but I guess I can tell you. The woman wrote a letter. It talked about a human beast that was unbeatable by humans. She said that it could take control of you and never release you from eternal pain. We did some investigating and found out that she was insane and she lived in that house alone because the doctor had told her to do so. I think that maybe she was the thing you hit and she some how survived and got back into her room before she died."

"And how it that possible?"

"Do you believe in demons, Mr. Scott?" asked Detective Roy, leaning forward as if to push out an answer.

"No, I don't," said Kevin, giving the detective a slight glare. He had been terrified by the detective's words. Images had shot up into the front of his mind that he now couldn't get out. He had thought that the detective was going to say something about him being in the house. He thought that they might have already known that he had been there and were just waiting for him to confess. He tried to stay calm but his legs started to shake under the table and he moved them so he wouldn't hit the detective. He didn't know what else to say and the detectives just sat there looking at him as if they were waiting for him to say something. Then there was a knock on the door.

"Yes, who's there?" said Kevin as calmly as he could. "It's me, honey. Can I come in?" said Samantha.

"Yes." She opened the door and brought in a plate of fried chicken. Kevin was grateful that she had come when she did. He couldn't take another minute of the talking to those men. He just wanted them to leave and forget about him. He just hoped that he hadn't left any fingerprints inside of Rachael's house. As he thought about all of this his wife had laid the plate on the table, and his head started to hurt. It was as if a sharp knife had cut threw his scalp, like someone had just shot him through his head with a shotgun, or like someone had thrown him on the ground and then they had beaten him on the head with a sledgehammer. He screamed out in pain and his wife came over to him and kneeled down. He put her hand on his back and rubbed it for a moment and then she asked him if he was okay. He didn't reply and started to breathe hard like he had asthma or some kind of breathing disorder.

"Is he okay?" asked Detective Roy.

"I don't know. Will you go into the living room and get his painkillers off of the table?" asked Samantha as she tried to help him in any way she could even though she knew nothing about what she was doing. Kevin continued to shake a little and then he placed his head on the table. He had felt some pain, but it wasn't anything he couldn't deal with. He wanted the detectives to leave so he could try to figure out what had really happened to him the day before. He knew that he had imagined things before, but they had never been anything like this. They had never resulted in someone dying or in him injuring himself. The only explanations that he made out of all of this was that he had finally gone insane, or that God wanted him to pay for doing what he had done. He had thought that it was all a dream and he never wanted to bring it up again but he thought that might just be the only way. He had read in the Bible that God forgives all who ask for it, but since that day his life had only gone from bad to worse and now he would soon be convicted of murder.

Soon the detective came back into the room with the painkillers and the children had heard the scream and followed him. At first they just stood by the door but when they saw that their father was hurt they crowded around the desk. Samantha quickly gave Kevin the medicine and then she started to pray. She put her head on the ground and prayed with all her soul for her husband to be okay. Kevin was still shaking with his head on the table and Samantha began to pray harder than she had ever prayed before and soon Kevin stopped. He looked up and took deep breaths to relieve himself. Samantha got up off of the ground and hugged her husband with a great smile on her face. She had prayed so hard that sweat was dripping off of her face and onto her husband. The detectives asked him if he was okay and then they left the room. They got inside of their car and drove off down the street.

"What do you think about him?" asked Lance.

"I think he did it," answered Roy.

"You mean that he killed the girl."

"Yes. All I need is some of his fingerprints."

"But why would he do it?"

"I don't know. We might have to look into this guy's background and find some kind of answers."

Kevin was fine now and his children were happy to see that he was okay. His wife was happy to have saved him with her prayer. Or so she thought.

"You see, Kevin. God still wants you to be one of his followers. You must come to church with me tonight," said Samantha, still hugging him. Kevin put his hand on his head and faked as if it still hurt.

"I'll have to come with you next Sunday. I don't think I'll stay awake today."

"But you promised. Please come with me?"

"Ya, Daddy. Come to church with us," said James, coming to sit on his father's knees. Kevin looked at him with a smile and then looked around the room at the rest of his children. He loved them all so much, including his wife, but he couldn't keep his promise today. He had too many things he had to think about, and to find answers for.

"Sorry, maybe next time. I mean I will come next time."

All the children were disappointed, but Kevin couldn't help but let them down this time.

"Alright, children. Go and get ready for church," said Samantha, sitting on Kevin's desk.

"All right, Mrs.," all of them said as they left the room. Once she was sure that they were gone, she jumped into Kevin's lap and started to kiss him. At first he just went with it, but at the time he really didn't want anything to do with her. She put her hand on his back and he acted as if that really hurt him. He was expecting it to, but was surprised because the day before it had hurt insufferably, but now he didn't feel anything. It was as if something had healed him of all of his pain in just a few hours. There wasn't even a petite amount of pain. He felt as if he could have jumped off of Mount Everest and fell into the ground face first and still gotten up and felt just as he had before he had jumped. Kevin didn't know why he was feeling this way and he thought it might be because he was still modestly drugged, but at the moment it didn't really matter. He just wanted to get away from Samantha.

"Sorry, I forgot about your hurt back," said Samantha as she rapidly pulled her hand off of Kevin's back.

"It's okay," said Kevin, still groaning, but starting to act as if he was feeling better. Samantha then got out of his lap and walked over to the door. She was about to leave when she turned around and looked at Kevin. Kevin looked back at her and tried to smile, but it didn't come out as he had planned. He couldn't understand it. His mouth just wouldn't form a smile in her direction. It was as if his entire body hated the one woman he would do anything for.

"What if I stay at home with you today?" asked Samantha with a very concerned look on her face. What she was concerned about will be left alone for now.

"No, you should go. I'll be fine," said Kevin, turning his head away. Even the very sight of her face was starting to upset Kevin. Samantha thought about it for a moment and then said she would go if he really wanted her to. Kevin was filled with blissfulness at the thought of her finally leaving the room. He couldn't have control of himself for much longer. For some reason it made him sick just to be around her, and just thinking about her created displeasure in his mind. He just wanted nothing to do with her. The one woman he had given up everything for and would do anything for was now something he wanted to be through with. He just couldn't understand. There had to be some kind of reason.

He had many questions and didn't know where to find the answers. He was lost like a dog that wouldn't use its nose to find its way home. He had no idea of how his pain had left him and it made no sense to him. He knew that the painkillers were supposed to help, but he had taken them before and they had never helped him like this. It wasn't that the pain had been compressed or hidden; it was gone. There wasn't a trace of pain anywhere and his body felt stronger than it had ever felt before. He was almost positive that he could get up at that very moment and grab a knife and stab himself and he wouldn't feel a thing. He was partly convinced that he should attempt his theory, but held himself back just to be on the safe side.

Once he was finished thinking about these things, Kevin got up out of his chair and walked to the living room. It looked as if Samantha had tried to clean up, but everything was still a mess. He sat down on the couch and turned on the TV. They had about two hundred channels, but all Kevin really watched was ESBN. He loved to watch football. He would have gone on to play college football, but he had to join the army so he could go to college and feed his family. At that time he had only one child. He didn't like to talk about it much because he had died. It was during the war and Kevin had to leave. He came back later to find out that he had been killed. The police could never tell him why and Samantha said that she had left him to go to the store to buy some food for him and came back and found him dead. His name was Robert, after Kevin's grandpa.

There was a football game on. It was a rerun between the Saints and the 49ers. Kevin had never lived in Louisiana and never wanted to, but had dreamed of taking the Saints to the Super Bowl. Someone had once told him that they had never been and that's when he made up his mind to work as hard as he could to lead them to a victory at the Super Bowl. He would wake up in the morning and work out, go to school and work out at football practice, and then work out when he got home. He didn't have time for anything else. That's all he wanted and he wasn't going to let anything stop him: not friends, not money, not girls, not anything. By the end of his junior years he was the strongest kid at his school and he had planned to go to Florida State to play football. During the summer is when he met Samantha. He had seen her around school, but never thought she was worth his time. He didn't think that he was too good for her or anything; he just thought that she wouldn't understand his dream and would want more attention than he could offer her. At school they had always worn uniforms and when Kevin saw Samantha at a party she almost took his breath away. She was the most beautiful woman he had ever seen. He couldn't understand why he loved her so much, he just couldn't control himself, he just had to have her belong to him. This party was the end of the year party and he had said that he would not go, because he had to work out, but he changed his mind for some reason and showed up. At first he hated it, but then he saw Samantha and thought it was his destiny for him to have gone. He knew just by looking at her that they were meant to be together. At first she wouldn't speak to him because she thought he was just a jock, trying to get laid; she wouldn't even give him her number and blew him off in front of everyone. He didn't care about getting embarrassed and continued on his quest to be with Samantha. He brought her flowers over the summer and had them delivered to her house. He gave up lots of his workout time to try to get her to talk to him, and she finally gave him her number; he called her twice every day. The first time was around noontime and the second was around ten in the evening. By the time school started again Kevin and Samantha had seen each other every day for about three weeks, and they were both very fond of each other. Kevin had given up much of his workout time and to make up for it he started taking steroids. He didn't care much about his own body or his own time he just wanted to be with Samantha. By the end of the year Samantha and Kevin had decided to get married. So they did that summer and moved into an apartment. About a year later Kevin was going to start going to college, but then Samantha got pregnant. Kevin had a job at Burger King, but he didn't think that would be good enough for him to take care of a family on, so he joined the army. He hated it the whole time, but he had to do it for his family. Soon the war came and he had to go. At first he was just going to try to get out of the army, but his wife told him to go; that he should fight for his country and keep it alive. He went and stayed over there for a year. He was on his way home when he got a call from Samantha. She told him about his son's death. He was angry with Samantha and soon he gave up going to church. He had still believed at that time but he wouldn't go to church unless it was Easter Sunday or something. Coming back from the war and seeing his son's death, he decided that he would never leave his family again. He dedicated everything to them; he never wanted to pursue his football dream ever again. The dream didn't mean much of anything anymore but he still felt like he could have done it.

Kevin sat on the couch absorbed within the TV dreaming of the life he should have had and still wished for. He knew that all dreams didn't come true and that some people made it and others didn't. He almost hated watching football because he knew that he was twice as good as everyone who stepped out onto that field. He knew he could have made a difference, but now it seemed too late.

"Goodbye, Daddy," said James as he gave Kevin a quick hug knocking him out of his trance.

"See you later, Father," said William as he walked out the door.

"See ya," said Keith as he followed William. Then Samantha came. She looked extremely lovely, but Kevin still didn't feel like talking to her. She was wearing a red dress that looked a little too flashy for church, but if Kevin was to say anything she would just say, "I don't know why you would care. You don't even come to church. It not about what you wear or what you come in. It's about your faith and the good things you do. You would know that if you would just come to church." They had had many arguments about church and they would always end in Samantha leaving to go to church and Kevin staying at home alone. Then he would go out to get her something that she would just say that she didn't need and wouldn't take. He would leave it for her on the table and in the morning she would be wearing or using whatever he got her.

Samantha walked over to Kevin and stood between him and the TV.

"I wish you would come," said Samantha with a smile on her face.

"I would if I could. I really don't feel good at all. I promise to come next week."

"You better keep your promise," said Samantha as she leaned forward and quickly kiss Kevin on the lips. "Well, we have to go. Keith is going to a party after church and William is going to the library. James and I were going to stay at church and wait until the evening service if that is all right with you."

"Yes, that's fine. I'll be okay on my own." He reached forward and grabbed Samantha by the waist. He put his head on her stomach and held her for a moment. It made him sick, like someone had poisoned him and made him throw up, like someone had taken his breath away and left him to die. He abhorred touching her. It was as if she was someone that he had hated for years when he had been in love with her instead. He had to use all of his strength to hold her for just a few seconds and after that he had to let her go.

"I'll see you later," she said as she left the house. Kevin was relieved that she had finally left. He just wanted to be away from her for some reason. It was just the other night when he would have done anything for her, but now he couldn't stand her. It just didn't make sense. There were times when he didn't want to be around her and he would force himself just to please her, but now he couldn't even do that. There had to be some kind of reason; he couldn't have just woken up this morning and hated the woman he gave up everything for. Kevin's head started to hurt again and he decided to go to sleep. He turned off the TV and then walked to his room. He threw himself onto his bed and tried to go to sleep. He lay there for about an hour turning from side to side trying to sleep, but he kept think of his wife. Every time he closed his eyes he saw her face. Her beautiful face seemed to haunt him. He longed for her, but didn't want her at the same time. He needed her, but couldn't have her because he feared what touching her might do to him; he loved and loathed her at the same time. Samantha's body was imprinted on the back of his eyelids. There was nothing that could have gotten her out of his mind.

He started to dream of Samantha. She was in the living room. There was only one couch and Kevin was nowhere to be found throughout the house. Samantha was holding a child it her arms. It had to be Robert. He was about six years old and wanted her to let him go so he could go somewhere and play. She told him that his father would be back soon and that she wanted him to be perfect for him when he got back; she didn't want him to be hurt or anything but perfect. He screamed and she finally let him go, but told him that he had to stay in the living room with her so she could watch him. He jumped off of her lap and started to play with his toys that were in the living room on the floor. Samantha watched him with great pleasure. She had the biggest smile Kevin had ever seen on her face. She looked as tranquil as a calm river. She looked as if nothing could have spoiled that moment for her. Then a knock came to the door. At first she didn't move, but then she thought maybe Kevin had gotten home early so she quickly answered the door. There was a black man standing there waiting for her. He was tall and wore very expensive clothes. Kevin would have though he was a pimp. He walked into the house without being invited. Samantha screamed something at him but Kevin couldn't hear anything. He turned and looked at her as if she was stupid and just walked farther into the house. Soon he was in the living room and he looked at Robert. Robert waved at him, but he didn't wave back. He just stood there for a moment and then he walked over to the couch and sat down. Samantha screamed some more, but he wasn't paying any attention to her; he was just watching Robert as he played. Samantha grew tired of yelling at him and she ran over to her son and picked him up. The man pointed his finger at her and said something. She quickly tired to walk out of the room, but the man quickly jumped in front of her; she tried to move him out of the way, but he hit her in the face and pulled Robert from out of her hands. Robert was screaming and crying for his mother, but he was too weak and helpless to do anything, but cry. Then the man placed Robert on the couch and walked over to Samantha; he kicked her in the stomach and then spit on her.

She couldn't do much of anything but just sit there and take it. The man then walked back over to Robert and tried to hug him, but he fought back as best as he could. The man didn't feel like fighting with him so he grabbed the pillow and put it over his head; he held it there for about thirty seconds and then took it off. Robert lay there not making a sound. Samantha tried to get up but she was in too much pain. The man pulled on her hair and threw her head into the wall. He came to grab her again but Samantha kicked at him and hit him in the balls. He fell and Samantha ran into the kitchen with the man close behind her. He reached at her and pulled her hair as she got into the kitchen. She slipped and fell on her back. The man rapidly kicked at her head and she tried to put her hands in the way of his blows. She spun herself so her feet were facing the man and kicked out as hard as she could.

He went back into the dining room table and fell from the pain of the blow. She got to her feet and opened the knife drawer and pulled out the sharpest knife she could find. The man was getting to his feet when Samantha stabbed him in the shoulder. He used his other foot to trip her and she fell onto the hard, marble floor. Then he picked her up by her hair and pulled her back to the living room. He threw her onto the carpet and then smiled at her. He walked up to her saying something as he shook the knife in her face. Samantha moved back so the knife wouldn't cut her, and she ran into the wall. The man stabbed at her, but he missed purposely just to frighten her. She put her head on the ground and cried. The man looked as if he got pleasure from seeing her cry. He left her and walked over to Robert. He had been unconscious while the man had beaten on Samantha. The man put the knife on Robert's neck and looked at Samantha. Then he stabbed Robert.

Kevin woke up as the knife went down into his son. His heart was beating rapidly. He would have woken up along time ago but something just wouldn't let him. He had never had such a terrifying dream. It all seemed so real. He had dreamed of his son's death hundreds of times. In all of those dreams he would see himself in his army uniform. He would just be getting off of the plane and then he would get into a cab. He would sleep most of the way to his house and he would wake up almost automatically as they drove up to his house; it was as if he had some kind of house sense that would tell him when he was at his home. He would get out of the car and look at his house. There would be policemen around his yard and the yellow tape that had caution written all on it. He would run up to the house and ask the police what happened. They would just move to the side and point to the door. Kevin would walk into the house and see more police that would point him throughout the house. Soon he would come to his son's room and Samantha would be on her knees outside of the door. She would have her hands on her face crying and the detective would point and tell Kevin to walk through the door. All this time, he would go through many different feeling; at first he thought maybe Samantha had been hurt and his son had been stolen or something. Then he thought maybe they both had been killed. He even thought that maybe Samantha had gone insane and killed Robert herself. Though, he loved them both he would have rather seen both of them dead than just his son. He couldn't understand how Samantha could have let something like this happen. Robert's body was torn apart; there was blood on the walls and everything was a mess. Kevin would have rather had someone come and kidnap his son than destroy his body and his entire life. That dream repeated into his mind ever since his son's death.

He had never seen that other dream and it troubled him. If that had happened why wouldn't Samantha have just told him the truth? Why would she hide that a man had killed Robert right in front of her? Why would she not tell the police? It just didn't make sense to him of why she would do something like that. If the man had killed Robert there, why wasn't there any blood? There would have been some kind of blood on the couch and there might have been a cut in the couch pillow or something. Kevin had never seen anything in the couch, not blood, not anything. He had never thought that Samantha's story about her going to the store and leaving him at home was true. He felt deep down that there had to be more than that to it but he just couldn't bring himself to speak to her about that day. There must have been something or someone who wanted him to know the truth.

Kevin got up out of the bed and took off his sweaty shirt. He never sweated in his sleep and now his shirt looked like he had jumped into a pool with it on. He quickly grabbed another shirt and then walked to the kitchen. The dream had made him feel weird. He wasn't hungry, but he thought that if he got something to eat it would make him feel better. His wife had cooked a lot of fried chicken and Kevin grabbed a beer and started to eat. He hadn't really eaten anything since the day before and he didn't feel even a little hungry. He ate the food quickly and soon he had drank the entire beer and eaten about six pieces of chicken. He knew that Samantha was a great cook, and that she could tame a wild beast with her food, but he could not taste anything. He thought that maybe it was from the painkillers and he didn't take much interest into the matter. He didn't feel like putting up with all of the stressful things that were going through his head so he decided to just get drunk. He grabbed another beer and sat back and drank it. When he was finished he felt the same as he had before he drunk it. He didn't feel any kind of sensation. There wasn't a buzz or anything. Usually, when he used to drink a lot, he would drink just one and be drunk enough to pass out. He felt good and in control. There wasn't any kind of drunkenness in him. He opened the refrigerator and took out the rest of the beers. Then he drank them one after the other. He still wasn't drunk. He felt the same. There wasn't any kind of change. He didn't even have to use the bathroom, and he had drunken about three gallons of beer. He got a trash bag and put all of the bottles in it. He didn't want Samantha to have to come home and fuss about him being drunk even though it looked as if that wouldn't happen. It was as if his body didn't need anything anymore.

Kevin told himself to stay calm. He just thought that must also be a side effect from using the painkillers. He just hoped it would wear off soon and he could get drunk and try to forget about life. He thought that maybe he should go and take a bath. He walked to the bathroom and turned on the shower. He always hated having to wait about a minute for the water to get hot and he left the bathroom and went to his room. He lied down on his bed to think. There were so many things going through his head, but that new dream was on the zenith of his thoughts. He couldn't think much of anything else. He felt that he had had a vision and someone wanted him to see the truth. He had to find a way to question Samantha about that day, but he knew if he brought it up she would only cry.

Kevin got up and walked back into the bathroom to take his shower. There was a leak in the sink and water was slipping out onto the floor. Kevin hadn't noticed it and he slipped as he was taking off his clothes. He hit his head on the side of the sink and fell onto the hard wet floor. He closed his eyes and tried to get ready for the pain that was going to come. He stayed there for about thirty second and the pain never came. He got to his feet and just shrugged his shoulders. He thought the he must have had some kind of super painkillers. He got into the shower and he couldn't feel if it was hot or cold. It wasn't even warm. There was just no feeling at all. It wasn't like when your foot falls asleep and your feeling kind of shaky; there was really no feeling at all.

Soon he grew tired of being in a shower that he couldn't feel and he got out and went back to his room to go to sleep. He had another dream. This one was more of a fantasy. Kevin saw himself in some kind of empty place. Everything was white. There wasn't anything, but Kevin inside of this place. Kevin couldn't ever see his shadow. He walked forward but seemed to go nowhere. It looked as if it was never-ending and that there was no way out. There wasn't a roof or a floor. If Kevin thought of going down then he would, but it would seem as if he hadn't moved at all. It was an endless maze that Kevin couldn't find the way out of. He began to panic. He didn't know where he was or how to get out. He couldn't even hear himself scream because there weren't any walls for the sound to bounce off of. Soon he started to feel at peace even though he was lost inside of some kind of blank space, and he almost wanted to just stay here forever.

He started to run straight even though he knew he wouldn't get anywhere something told him to just go. Soon he could see something off into the distance; he couldn't tell what it was. It was just a blur. He stopped to try to see what it was and the ground moved him closer to it. It was as if he was on a super, fast escalator. The object had been at least a mile away from him and he was next to it in about fifteen seconds. It was a table. A wooden table that was very shiny and looked brand-new. Kevin walked around the table and tried to decide if he should touch it or not. It looked real, but it could have been a trap. He made up his mind to just try and face what ever happened next. As he reached a chair came up from underneath him and he sat in it. It was a wooded chair just like the table and it moved so that Kevin was stuck between it and the table. He pushed back from the table but it would let him loose. Then he used his elbow and hit the chair trying to make it break, but there wasn't a chance of him even putting a bend in it. He would have had a better chance of breaking a diamond than denting that chair. Soon he just gave up. There wasn't much of anything he could do. Then the arm of the chair turned into a hand and grabbed Kevin's head. It pulled back and made him look up. There was another object and it was falling straight towards him face. He shook his head and tried to release himself, but it was hopeless. The object came down and hit him in the face.

Kevin woke up and put his hand on his head. He had a bad headache. He kept hearing knocking and he thought it was coming from the door. He waited until he was sure that it was the door and then he got up to answer it. He still felt strong and his stomach wasn't even a little upset. He could not remember a time when he had gone this long with food and not had an upset stomach. The person at the door knocked persistently. Kevin could tell just from that that they were very eager to see someone. He pulled the locked off the door and opened it to find the last person he had ever wanted to see.

It was John. The man from the Wal-Mart Kevin had last worked at. He felt a little afraid. This man was a stranger to him and he had never seen him before until the Wal-Mart, but he knew where he lived. He must have stalked him, and that would mean that he was a professional because Kevin hadn't lost his army abilities and could have easily noticed if someone was following him. He could be a rapist and have been trying to kill Kevin and his family or just a serial killer picking out his next victims. Kevin didn't know what to think. He wanted to just shut the door and lock it but he didn't want the man to think that he was afraid. He thought the best thing to do was just to act like he didn't know him.

"Hello, sir," said Kevin. "Can I help you with something?"

"Yes, my name is John. Do you remember me?"

"Well, not really. Why, should I?"

"I talked to you at the store the day you had that accident. I prayed for you, are you alright?"

"Yes, I'm fine, but I don't see why you should concern yourself with me. I think you would have better things to do."

"I know it's strange for me, being a stranger, to be concerned about you but I have something to tell you that I think you should know."

"Yes, well you wait here a moment," said Kevin as he shut the door. He didn't know who this man was, but he wasn't going to stand there and believe that he was worried about him when he didn't even know him. Kevin was now certain that he didn't know him and had never seen anyone else in his life that could have resembled him. He concluded that the man had to be insane and all he had to do was show him that he wasn't into playing games. He quickly went into this room and looked for his shotgun. He had put it in his closet the last time he used it, but it wasn't there. He threw everything out of it and looked again to find nothing. He didn't see why anyone would have had to touch it other than himself, and he grew angry when he couldn't find it in the place that he knew he had laid it. Before he got entirely irate he counted to ten and then looked under his bed. There it was. He didn't think about how it had gotten there, and why it was there didn't bother him. He quickly pulled it from under the bed and loaded it. He didn't plan on shooting the gun but he knew that if he had to he would. He could always say that the man was a stranger and that he was trespassing. He was sure that the law wouldn't mind him killing that man.

He went back to the front door and kicked it open, almost hitting John in the face. He then quickly pointed the gun at him. John put his hands up and backed slowly down the path and away from the house. Kevin came slowly out of the house ready to pull the trigger.

"What do you want from me?" asked Kevin with an irate tone.

"I told you," said John, backing up into his car. "I have to tell you something that I think you should know."

"No you don't have to tell me anything, but I have something to tell you! I don't ever want to see you around my house again, and if I do you will not live to see another day." Kevin put the gun right in his face to let him know that he was serious.

"Sir…Uh…Kevin, there's no need for all of this," said John as he moved back a little.

"How do you know my name?"

"I know your wife," said John, trying to make a friendly face.

"What?" Kevin rushed at John and hit him with the butt of the gun. John fell to the ground, because the gun hit him in the stomach and knocked the wind out of him.

"I don't know what the hell is wrong with you but I don't ever want to see you again. You're lucky I haven't called the police." Then it came to Kevin. Why didn't he want to call the police? Was it because he didn't want to talk to them or did he have some kind of pity for this man that he thought was trying to kill him? A sane man would have called the police in the first place, but Kevin felt that sanity had left him a long time ago.

"Hurry up and get out of here," said Kevin, pointing the gun at him. John looked up with a smile on his face and then got to his feet.

"I see that you're not in a good mood. I'd tell you that I would come back later, but I think you might shoot me. Here, I shall give you a card, which you can use to reach me if you want to talk." He pulled a card out from his pocket and tried to give it to Kevin, but he wouldn't take it. Soon John just placed it on the ground.

"You should control you temper more," said John, getting into his car. "Not all people are as generous and helpful as me. I wish you the best in your recovery."

"Get out of here and don't let me see you again!" Then John drove out of the driveway and down the road. When Kevin was sure he was gone, he started to walk back up to his house, but before he reached the door he heard a voice. He couldn't tell where it was coming from and it sounded as if it was coming from all directions at once. It kept repeating itself about every five seconds and echoed on until the next one came. It continued to say the same five words. "Why didn't you shoot him? Why didn't you shoot him? Why didn't you shoot him?" It got so loud that Kevin couldn't even hear the sound of his own mind and he was almost paralyzed by the words. He really didn't know why he didn't shoot him. He didn't even know the man and he certainly didn't believe in God, so what did he have to worry about? Soon the voices stopped, but Kevin was still traumatized.

Kevin ran into the house and closed the door with shaky hands. He looked at the clock and it read 3:30. He knew that his wife would be home soon and he would ask her about this man named John. It hurt him to think of how she might know him. The thought of her cheating on him was impulsive. He could not stand to think that she had done such a horrible thing to him. If she had he would never forgive her. He wouldn't know how. All he would be able to do was curse her. She talked so much about her God and her rules and morals; she talked so much about her fortune in Heaven and how she wished he would join her there one day. She once told him that she could not bear the thought of living with such a sinning husband. She had talked so much about his sin and the things that he was doing wrong that if she cheated on him she would have gone against everything she had ever told him. She would just be proving that life has no meaning and that he shouldn't waste his time trying to provide for his family; instead he should have just committed suicide a long time ago because with out his family he was only living for nothing and he had no purpose, even though the way he was living didn't have much of a purpose anyways.

Kevin placed his head against the door and let a few tears escape from his eyes. He generally wasn't the brand of person that would allow himself to cry, but he felt too baffled and perplexed to know what to do. All he felt like he could do was cry. His mind was just swathed into hundreds of thoughts that all seemed to lead either to nowhere or into another inspiration that would just continue on forever. He could not bring himself to find an answer to any of his questions. If there was one his mind was too feeble to grasp it and hurt from just trying to think about it. He imagined that if he felt this much pain just thinking about it he might be better off never knowing anything at all. What was the point of knowing something if you had to suffer constantly because of it? Soon Kevin concluded that it was pointless and forced himself to stop crying.

When he was finished he went back into this room and put the gun back underneath his bed. He was going to act like he had never used it and then ask Samantha about why it had been moved. He started to think about the answer to that question, but he stopped himself. He wasn't feeling like going through any pain and now that he thought about it he had only imagined the pain in the first place. He still couldn't feel anything. Nothing. He was sure that there was something wrong now and that the painkillers had nothing to do with what was happening. Kevin didn't want to think about anything at the time, but he had to try something to see if he really could feel or not.

The kitchen was the place to start. Kevin had thought about it and almost stopped himself from walking into the kitchen but the urge was too strong. He just had to know. He could stand going another minute not knowing if he could feel or not. *Maybe I really can and I was imagining that I couldn't,* thought Kevin as he opened a drawer. This was something that he had never thought that he would be doing. He hated sharp objects and of all of them the knife was the one he hated the most. He didn't know why he felt this way, but a shrink had once told him that it was possible that because his father had used a knife in killing all of his victims this had caused him to have a fear of them. Either way Kevin hated knives and would never have thought that he would be using one voluntary on himself.

Slowly Kevin tried to place the knife against his skin, but he just couldn't bring himself to do it. He kept repeating in his mind, *I can't feel it. I can't feel it. I can't feel it. I can't…*but even that could not get him to do it. He felt like such a coward not being able to even poke himself with a knife. He had been in the war and had faced hundreds of traps and other weapons far worse than a knife, but the moment someone pulled out a knife on him he froze like a statute. If it weren't for a landmine being between him and his enemy he would not be standing in the kitchen now.

Soon Kevin heard a car drive by and he was in such profound thought that he jumped and stabbed himself in the arm. His first reaction was to jump and squeal but there wasn't any pain. Nothing. He did not feel any blood coming out nor did he feel anything that was remotely close to pain. He didn't know what to do. He just stood there and looked at his arm. He didn't know if it was best to leave the knife where it was or to take it out. Then he thought that Samantha would be sure to say something if she came home and saw the knife hanging from his arm. He gripped the knife firmly and slowly pulled it out. It wasn't that deep of a cut, but it was deep enough for blood to have come out and Kevin moved his face as far as he could from his hand so he wouldn't get blood all over him. He didn't have to worry because nothing came out. Not even one drop. It was as if he hadn't even pierced himself or something had healed him before he had a chance to look because there was nothing there. Not even the slightest sight of the knife even having entered Kevin's skin. His hand was fine.

Now Kevin was sure that he had just been dreaming. He told himself that he was just imagining that he had stabbed himself and he hadn't really done it. If he had there would have been blood or something on the knife and there was nothing. What he had been seeing was impossible and there was no way he could not have any feeling within his entire body. He reminded himself of all of the hatred he had felt towards Samantha and told himself that even that could not have been real. All he had to do was go sit down and wait for himself to wake up. Though he didn't believe in God or in any other kind of religion he knew one thing for sure. What was happening to him only happened to insane people and he definitely wasn't insane.

Kevin walked back into the front of the house and sat down on the couch. Everything wasn't making any sense to him. He knew that the painkillers were not keeping him from being hungry; it had to be something else. He thought about the old woman. He hoped that she was gone, but knew it wasn't true. She had said that she would see him soon, and he was sure that she intended to do so. He didn't know what she was. She could be a demon, or even an angel, but Kevin told himself that he didn't believe in such thing and he quickly forgot about that theory. He then suspected that she was just a figment of his imagination like everything else that was happening. That would explain why the cut on his hand had disappeared. His only problem was that everything that was happening seemed real.

He remembered one time when he was young and he was living with his grandparents. He had had a nightmare. He saw himself in his yard playing with his friends and family. It must have been his birthday or something because he was the center of the attention. Everyone was trying to talk to him or be his friend and he just walked around smiling. The party was in the back yard and Kevin drifted away from the party and into the front of the house to be alone. He was happier than he could ever remember himself being. He wished that this day would stay with him forever and he would live life with no worries. He thought that he had to be in a dream because life in the real world could never allow anyone to be as happy as he was. He felt so pleased from the party that he could have taken all of the happiness inside of him and fueled a hot air balloon long enough for him to fly around the world for years.

He sat in the front thinking to himself and then he noticed a truck coming up the street. It was old and looked very rusty and as if it would stop at any minute. Soon it came to Kevin's yard and stopped. A woman came out from the car and looked around the yard. Kevin could tell that she was white, but her face was a blur. She walked over to a tree and pointed at Kevin. She then gave a gesture that induced that she wanted Kevin to come over to her, and he didn't see why he shouldn't so he went. He got about five feet in front of her and he felt like he was in some kind of danger. He didn't know what it was but something told him to run and he turned and tried to. He didn't get very far; there was a stick next to the tree and the woman picked it up and threw it at his back as he tried to run. It went through his body and it pinned him to the ground. Then the woman walked to the front of him and walked into his house leaving him in the yard. Soon after she had gone in the house caught on fire and Kevin would wake up from the dream.

Kevin got an idea after reliving the dream. He thought that maybe the woman and in his dream was the same woman he had seen at Rachel's house. As he was thinking about this he heard the same voice from earlier start talking to him again. This time he was sure that it was coming straight from his head.

"You could have killed him," said the voice.

"What," said Kevin, being interrupted from his thoughts.

"You could kill him and anyone else you want."

"Who are you? What do you want?"

"I want you, Kevin. I told you we would talk."

"You…You're the old lady."

"You'll find out soon enough," said the voice as it drifted away. Kevin thought it was gone and then a loud slamming sound came into his ear. He thought it had burst his eardrum and he covered his ear. The pain left just as Samantha walked into the house. James followed her.

"Hey, how are you doing?" asked Samantha as she put her keys on the key rack.

"I'm fine," said Kevin, quickly putting his hand down from his ears. "How was church?"

"It was good. You should have come. The sermon was great and you might have learned something about what is really important. What have you been doing all of this time?"

"Nothing. Just sleeping. There isn't much that I can do anyways," said Kevin as he got up and started to walk to his room. He tried to walk as if he was hurt so Samantha wouldn't talk to him anymore about church. He was just passing Samantha and on his way to his room when James stopped him and gave him a hug. Kevin tried to make it look as if it hurt, but he didn't do that good of a job. He hoped that Samantha wouldn't notice.

"Where are you going now?" asked Samantha as she was putting her purse on the table. She gave Kevin a look as if to say something was wrong, but then she figured he was just still hurt and let it go.

"I'm still tired. I think I would feel better just sitting in my room," said Kevin as he started to walk father down the hall.

"Okay. I hope you feel better soon. Do you want me to come and lay with you?" asked Samantha as she started to follow him.

"No, I don't want to worry you. And—" The phone rang and cut Kevin off. Samantha quickly forgot about Kevin and ran to answer the phone. It was one of her friends and soon she was absorbed into a conversion. If Kevin had believed in God this would have been another time he would have thanked him, but instead he thought he should thank the person whom invented the phone. He didn't know who that was, but if he had lived in his time he would have walked for miles just to kiss him or her and say, "Thank you."

Kevin walked to his room and sat on his bed. He turned on his TV but he could not watch it. He kept thinking that Samantha might be cheating on him and he couldn't live with himself if that was true. He thought that maybe all of his worrying about his wife had caused him to think up this old lady that he had seen in one of his dreams. He knew that he had to talk to Samantha about all of this, but he feared that the truth might not be what he wanted to hear. What if she was cheating? He didn't know what he would do and he tried not to even think about it but he couldn't stop himself. He loved her almost as much as she loved her God. He sometimes wished that she would treat him as she did God, but he knew that would never happen unless he somehow showed her the truth about God. In this case neither of them knew a thing about that.

Samantha came into the room shortly after he had entered, but she changed and left without saying a word. She had looked at him once or twice, but didn't do anything. He had wanted to say something, but he couldn't bring himself to say it. He thought that it might be best to just wait until that night to talk about it so he wouldn't worry his children hearing anything. She looked as if she was in a hurry and quickly wanted to get out of the room. Once she was gone Kevin heard the door close, the car start, and then the car going down the driveway. Kevin screamed James' name to see if he was still in the house but he wasn't. Once again Kevin was alone inside of the house.

Kevin tired to go to sleep, but the very same moment he closed his eyes there was a noise that startled him. It sounded like something in the kitchen had fallen. Kevin wanted to get up and go look, but he told himself that he most likely imagined it and that he should just go to sleep and try to forget about it. That's what he was going to do when he heard another sound louder than the first one. This one frightened Kevin and he almost couldn't move. He then told himself that he had been to war and back so he shouldn't be afraid of any intruder or thief that had broken into his house.

Kevin took a deep breath and then reached under his bed for his gun. He then reloaded it and started his way out of his room. As he walked down the hall the noises seemed to increases. They didn't get any louder, but faster. He could not tell what was making the sound, but he knew it was coming from the kitchen. Soon he was at the end of the hall and he stopped for a moment. He knew that once he walked past the door he would come in contact with whatever was inside of his house. There was something inside of him that was telling him to go back, but he told himself that only a fool would do something like that. He was a man and was not going to hack down. He would kill what ever it was because this was his house and he owned everything in it. There was nothing inside of his house that could kill him before he could get a shot off and if he died as well then at least he would die a man.

What Kevin found beyond that door was something he almost couldn't believe. There was a man in his kitchen that was breaking the dishes with a hammer. He would break one and then quickly move on to the next one with out stopping to look around or anything. It was as if he had a mission and there was nothing that was going to stop him. Nothing. Kevin didn't want to startle him because he thought that he must have been insane so he slowly walked towards the kitchen with his gun ready to shoot at a moment's notice. Kevin was about a foot behind the man before he noticed that Kevin had been watching him. As the man turned around Kevin was so terrified that he didn't know what to do with him. This man was an evil being that would forever haunt him in every way. He was something that he would never completely rid himself of and wanted nothing to do with. It was his father.

Kevin couldn't move. His hands were frozen. Mark just looked at Kevin and smiled. He then broke one more plate before he walked over to Kevin. The entire time he just stood there and looked at him. Kevin couldn't believe that he was walking. He had made sure that he had paralyzed him, but now he was right in front of him moving as if nothing had ever happened.

"You look surprised," said Mark as he continued to move closer and closer to Kevin's frozen body. "You should have known that I was going to come back for you. I wasn't just going to let you stab me and then get away with it. You're such a fool. You're a waste of time. Allow me to finish you." Mark then pulled the gun from Kevin's hands and then hit him in the jaw causing him to fly into the air and onto the dinning room table that was behind him. That knocked Kevin out of his trance. Luckily he couldn't feel anything. Once Kevin hit the table Mark took the gun and started to swing it at Kevin. Kevin quickly moved his hands in the way of each blow. If he had been himself he would have been in great pain, but once again he couldn't feel.

Mark continued to hit Kevin for about thirty more seconds and then he twisted the gun so that the butt of the gun was facing Kevin's stomach. Then with great lighting speed he brought the gun down hard enough to make blood come flying out of Kevin's mouth and onto Mark's face. Kevin took this opportunity to get up and attack Mark because the blood had blinded him for the moment. Kevin used all of his strength and knocked Mark back into the counter making him scream in pain. Kevin then ran into the kitchen and grabbed a knife off of the counter and turned around just in time to keep Mark from hitting him. He had dropped the gun and was almost helpless to Kevin at the moment. Kevin thought that he should have just lunged out and killed him, but he wanted to know what he was doing inside of his house.

"It's been a long time," said Kevin, watching Mark very closely. If there was one moment that Kevin even thought he was going to try to attack him he was going to make sure he clouted him first. Kevin remembered that his father was a killing machine and unless he moved almost a second before he did it would be very unlikely that he would survive for very long.

"Yes, you're right," said Mark in a very serene voice as if he was much more superior then Kevin. "It has been a while. I have to say that I've almost missed you. I don't know why I allowed you to harm me before, but it will not happen twice. You will die here in this very room and I will not let you live. You will feel my fury and pain, and once I'm finished with you I will murder your entire family and burn their bodies. There will not be anything left for anyone to find."

"What do you get out of this? What is the point of you killing me? You're the one who had me and brought me into this world."

"That was my mistake and I am here to fix it. I will correct the errors that I have made and will not allow you to live." Then Mark quickly ripped off his shirt and threw it at Kevin. Kevin didn't have much time to think, but he managed to dunk under it and throw the knife at his knees. It went through completely and stuck into the cabinet door behind Mark. Mark screamed and fell to the side, but grabbed the counter before he hit the ground. Kevin then managed to crawl by Mark and make his way towards the gun. Once there, Kevin then picked it up and aimed it at Mark, but never had time to get the bullet out of the gun. While he was pulling the trigger, Mark picked up another knife off of the counter and threw it right at the mouth of the gun. This caused a huge explosion that sent Kevin through the wall that separated the kitchen and the living room, and it sent Mark flying into the sink.

Kevin got to his feet quickly and noticed that he had many wounds and he was losing a lot of blood. There were also pieces of the gun everywhere a few were stuck in Kevin's skin. Once he pulled out all of the gun pieces he then started to limp over to where Mark was. Mark was screaming because of the pain he was in. He had landed on everything that was inside of the sink. There were knife and forks and lots of other sharp objects that had pierced his skin and were causing him to lose a lot of his blood. Kevin looked at him and he wanted to laugh. He was now thankful that he couldn't feel anything that his father had done to him, but that his father could feel everything that he was receiving. He wanted Mark to suffer until he got tired of it and then he would terminate him and disregard everything that he had ever done to him.

Kevin then grabbed a sharp piece of metal off of the ground and continued to limp closer and closer to his helpless foe. Once Kevin was over him he just looked down and laughed again. Mark didn't even notice him and just continued to scream. Kevin then started to remember all of the horrible things he had done. All of the pain he had caused him and all the wrong he had done. It didn't matter to Kevin that he was doing something bad, but it was just that he had mess up his life and that was something he hated. People who knew would always look at you as if you would turn out doing those same things when that's not how it is at all. Instead, Kevin had fought his entire life trying not to be like his father.

Kevin lifted the knife over his head and didn't have to think twice about what he was going to do. Once he made up his mind he got to work. He stabbed Mark over and over again. There was nothing that was going to stop him and he wouldn't let anything stop him. This time he was going to make sure that his father would never come back again and that this would be the end of him. Soon Kevin could no longer hear him screaming and he was covered in blood. He had to take deep breaths to calm himself down and then he started to limp towards the phone so he could call the police. As he picked up the phone Mark got up out of the sink. Everything that had stabbed him while he was in the sink was still attached to him and he looked as if he was no longer in any pain, even though it was hard to see his face. Kevin had cut most of it up, but he still managed to form a smile. Kevin had heard him move and quickly turned around in amazement. He couldn't believe that now he had failed twice in killing his father. The hatred just took over Kevin and he charged at Mark. Right before he hit him, Mark opened his mouth and shot this black glob out of his mouth and it attached to Kevin's face and started to suffocate him. He tried to fight back but there was nothing he could do. This was the end.

A few moments later, Kevin found himself alone in the kitchen. He was lying on the floor and he thought that he had been sleeping because he had drool coming down his face. Kevin started to push himself off of the ground and found it to be an intricate task. He still couldn't feel, but he had worked out enough to be able to imagine how his body was feeling. It was as if he had just spent the last few hours lifting weights, or fighting someone. Though he had to struggle, Kevin soon got to his feet and looked around. Everything looked as it had been and there was no trace of anyone having come into the house. Kevin was so confused that he didn't know what to do. He knew that what had just happened to him was more than just a dream. He had never in his life dreamed about his father and he didn't see why he should dream about him now. Why after all of those years would he finally dream of the one person that he wanted to forget about?

He walked back to his room and lay down again. He quickly put his head under his pillow and began to do something that he was always told no man ever does. Cry. He cried as if he was a kid that had lost his favorite toy and looked everywhere, but found nothing. That was how Kevin was feeling at the time. He had looked everywhere for the answers to his questions and found nothing. There was nothing he could do but cry.

Soon Samantha came home and she quietly walked into the room and changed clothes. Kevin had still been crying, even though the entire time he didn't feel as if he was doing much of anything, but as Samantha walked into the room he stopped so she would not be worried about him or come and touch him. She left the room without saying a word and Kevin didn't hear from her again until she called him for dinner. Kevin told her that he had already eaten and she left him alone for a while longer. Kevin was fearful of what might happen if he went to sleep so he just stayed awake. He could only think of his father and of the other uncanny things that had been happening to him. If anyone would have come up to him and told him that something like this was happening to them, he would have never believed them. He would have gone behind their back and laughed at them as if they were a fool. He would have looked at them as a fool for the rest of their life and would have never allowed them to live it down. In his world things like this never happened and even though it was happening to him now he still couldn't believe it and wasn't going to.

He just stayed awake until the night came. That was about seven hours later and Kevin didn't feel even a little tired but he quickly acted as if he had fallen asleep as Samantha came into the room to go to bed. She didn't get straight into bed. First she took off her clothes and walked into the bathroom. Kevin had seen her do this and he knew that the only time that happened was when she wanted sex, or to make love as she would say. The very thought of that made Kevin's heart ache, and this was very painful because he hadn't felt anything else for the last few days. It came as if someone had shot him with a bullet and he almost screamed out. He had to use all of his strength to keep himself from doing it and he didn't have much to begin with. Soon the pain left and Kevin returned to being emotionless. That was about the time that Samantha came out of the bathroom and jumped into the bed. Kevin moved quickly so that she wouldn't touch him as she bounced and then just closed his eyes and tried to act like he was asleep, but Samantha knew he was awake.

"Hey, honey. What's wrong with you?" said Samantha, putting her leg around Kevin's back.

"Nothing, I'm still tired," mustered Kevin, just barely being able to say anything. His body was burning from her touch. It was as if he was lying in lava, or like he was walking across hot coals. He moved so she would slide off of him and then turned and looked at her.

"You know my back is still hurt," said Kevin, trying not to sound too angry, but he couldn't help it. He wanted nothing to do with this woman and he had no reasonable reason why. There were other reasons that Kevin could think of but he had decided to declare them entirely false. If he couldn't prove them then they meant nothing, and nothing was just simply that. Nothing.

"I'm sorry," said Samantha with a sigh. "I'll just go to bed. I'll pray for you. I hope you feel better in the morning." Then she rolled over to her side and let out a sigh just to bother Kevin. Usually that would have worked, but at the time he really didn't care. It would have been much simpler for him to just have killed her and had nothing to worry about then to try to please her. What did it matter?

That's what you should have done in the first place, thought Kevin as a smile came to his face. If only he could get her to leave the room, that would have made his day, but he still had other things to attend to. He knew that now would be the best time for him to bring up John. He just hoped that things wouldn't turn out as bad as he thought they would. Well, if they did it might just help him figure things out. Either way it had to be discussed, and he couldn't go another moment without saying something.

"So how was your day?" ask Kevin, trying to sound like he cared, which was extremely hard for him to do at the moment.

"It was just fine. I might have been better if you would have come to church with us. You might have liked the service to day. There was free food, many of your old friends are starting to show up and miracles are happening. This world is changing and I don't want you to get left behind, Kevin. But you make your own choices and there is nothing that I can do to change your mind. What will you do when you look up one day and God has taken everything away from you and there is nothing left for you? The end will come, Kevin, and you'll be lost if you don't find the light."

"Why didn't you tell me that? I would have gone then. Of course I would feel fine going to church and serving something that has never done anything for me; something that is too afraid to even show its face; something that has been written about and only witnessed by fools. If I allowed myself to be such a fool then I would have died years ago, and what good would that have done me?" This entire time Samantha had said nothing and not even moved. It was as if Kevin's words had killed her, but he wasn't done yet. "Even it there is a God and he created all things to serve him and worship him, what would be the point of my life in doing such a thing as that. I would only become a robot or something and spend all of my life under something else's control. That would truly be a waste of time. Are you sure that where you're going is light or is that just something you've imagine and hope for? What will you do when you come to find nothing?"

Samantha tried to say something, but she almost cried as it came out so she waited a moment and then spoke.

"You have no faith and your judgment will come, and then there will be nothing I can do for you." She then put her head under her pillow and started to cry. Usually this would have made Kevin feel bad but now he was enjoying it. He didn't know why, but it felt almost as good as sex sitting they're watching her cry. A wise man would have noticed that his feelings had come back, but that wasn't anything that he could comprehend at the time.

Though Kevin was enjoying his time he had to still get some information out of her.

"Samantha, I don't want to talk about that any more. Maybe you're right and I just haven't seen the light yet. I'll try harder to believe, okay. To tell you the truth I should have gone today. I really wasn't feeling that bad."

"I knew you were faking," said Samantha as she turned around and pointed her finger at Kevin. "I should have dragged you down to the church. I cannot believe you would lie to me about something like that. That's why you need to go to church now." She continued screaming and fussing for sometime while Kevin just pretended to smiled at her.

"What do you think is so funny?" asked Samantha as she stopped fussing and looked right in his face.

"I was just messing with you. I really am in a lot of pain." *Lie.* "I really want to start going to church." *Lie.* "I am going to start next week." *Lie.* "I promise." *Lie.* The word lie continued to repeat in his head after every lie he just told his wife. He shut his eyes and tried to block it out as his wife hugged him. The hug felt like someone had just laid a huge block on Kevin's chest and he couldn't breathe. He was about to push her off when she left him go.

"You better keep your promise. I'm not going to let you go back on your word," said Samantha, allowing a smile to come to her face.

"I promise," said Kevin, turning to his side.

"Okay. I hope you'll feel better tomorrow. I'm going to wake up early and cook you whatever you want. What do you want?" asked Samantha with much excitement in her voice.

"I don't know. I love everything you cook."

"So it will be a surprise and don't come to me tomorrow complaining about what you wanted to eat."

"I won't." Then they both stopped talking and Kevin desperately wanted to bring up John, but he didn't know how. At first he thought it might just be easier just asking her if she was cheating on him and demand an answer, but he knew that then she would either cry and leave or tell him that she didn't know what he was talking about and leave. Why would she tell him if she was cheating on him? So after that he thought he should ask her if she knew someone named John, but he wasn't sure if that would work because if she was cheating on him then she would act as if she didn't know anyone by that name and then she would know that he knew. So he did the next best thing.

"Hey, someone came here earlier looking for you. I didn't know him and I told him I would tell you that he come."

"Who?"

"It was a man named John something," said Kevin, trying to sound as composed and susceptible as he could.

"John?" She was quiet for a moment.

"John. What did he look like?" she asked this as if she was hoping that Kevin would describe someone other than the person she was thinking of.

"He was white and kind of short. He had a gold watch on. I only remember that because it was ugly. His hair was black and he looked like he was young."

"There was a John that used to go to our church, but I don't know why he would want to come and talk to me. I only spoke to him a couple of times while he was there."

"What happened to him?"

"Well, he just stopped coming one day. He said it was something about us having false teachings and sinful ways. No one believed him though because there was this other guy named Carlos and you would never see those two apart from on another. Everyone thought they were gay; they went to the bathroom together and everything. If anyone has sinful ways it would have been him. I mean we accepted him into our church and our home and then he went around talking bad about us. Things like that don't happen around here. You are either a part of the church or not. There is no in between."

"Well, why do you think he wanted to see you?"

"I couldn't tell you. He left the church about two weeks ago, and I haven't seen or heard of him since. We used to be friends in the church, I mean that we were family and loved one another, but after he left, he never talked to me again. I thought he had moved or something. I guess he just wanted someone to talk to." Kevin was relieved because she sounded as if she was telling the truth, and that was almost exactly what he wanted to hear. He decided to wait until the morning to ask Samantha about why the gun had been moved.

That night he slept peacefully for the first time since the accident. He couldn't even remember having a dream. It took him a few hours because he was afraid of what he might see. Every time Samantha rolled over and touched him a sharp pain went up his back and woke him up. He was glad when she had got up to go and fix him breakfast and he just laid there until she came back with his food. She had made him some chocolate chip pancakes, which were his favorite, and some bacon. He smiled at her, but wasn't happy to see her and asked her to let him eat alone. She said that she couldn't eat with him anyways because she had to get James ready for school. He stared to eat his food, but he still wasn't hungry and that was bothering him. He had to find some answer today. He didn't know how but he knew he would.

Kevin then started to notice the wounds on his body. He had remembered that when he was in the hospital that they had seemed bad, but now there was nothing. Every wound that he had received in the crash was gone and he looked as if nothing had ever happened. He was really starting to think that maybe everything that he was seeing and that was happening had been real; that his father had really came into his home and tried to kill him; that all of this had to do with something that he chose not to believe in and would have nothing to do with.

After he was finished thinking, he got up out of his bed and went into the bathroom to change. He quickly examined the rest of his body just to make sure that all of his wounds were gone and then he put on his clothes and left the bathroom. Once back into his room he started to put the covers on his bed. This was something that he always did because his grandmother had always told him to do so. As he was doing this, the covers almost jumped up out of the bed and enclosed him. He didn't have time to do much of anything before the covers pulled him to his bed and trapped him between it and the mattress. Kevin struggled but he couldn't get free. Soon he saw someone above him. He couldn't see who it was because of the covers and it looked like some kind of outline to Kevin. He was going to scream out when the banshee spoke first.

"Hello, how are you doing down there. Do you want to get that off?" said the banshee, looking down at him.

"What, yes of course I want this off. Why wouldn't I?" said Kevin still try to free himself.

"I can help you. Do you want help?" said the banshee in a different voice from the first one. This one was more of a vice-like voice.

"Yes, want do you think you can do?" asked Kevin, not really worried about the figure.

"I can help you to do many things if you allow me to, but it is all up to you. Without your consent I can do nothing," said the banshee switching back to the first voice, which sounded very sweet and kind.

"Well, I would like it if you helped me out of here. I…" But Kevin was starting to lose air and he could no longer breathe.

"Ha, it seems as if you do need me. If you want help all you have to do is raise your right hand and you'll be set free," said the banshee, switching back to the vice voice. Kevin then tried to raise his hand, but he couldn't move it. It was either because the cover had gotten tighter or because he was losing his strength because the air supply was gone and he would soon die. Dying was something that Kevin really wasn't looking forward to. There was no reason why he should. He had nothing to hope for except to just disappear and become nothing. He wasn't ready to let that happen. He knew that one day his time would come, but he wasn't going to let it be today. He used all of the strength that he could muster and fainted as he raised his hand and gave in to the banshee.

He hadn't fainted for long before he awoke and he could feel his strength and everything coming back to him. He didn't know how or why, but the covers started to return to normal and he was safe.

"How did you do that?" said Kevin, astounded, but no one answered him. The only thing that made sense to him about all the weird stuff was that the old lady was doing it, and that she must have been the one that was above the covers talking to him. He decided to just let her come forward and tell him what she wanted. He knew that she wanted something from him and that he wasn't going to find out until she wanted him to know. All he had to do was act as if he didn't care and as if he was a slave and then he could figure out a way to beat her at her own game and return his life back to normal. All he had to do was wait.

Once Kevin had caught his breath and regained his composure he continued to eat his tasteless breakfast. For all he knew he could have been stuffing clay down his throat. It wouldn't have made any difference to him because he wasn't hungry anyways. He was just trying to please Samantha so she would not whine and complain about him not eating anything. Then she would want him to go to the doctor again and he really didn't want to waste his time doing such a thing. The more he thought about it the more senseless Samantha seemed to him. He couldn't understand how he had changed into this person he was now. There was a time that he would have fought anything for her, but now he didn't even want to talk to her. All of these thoughts started to hurt his head, so he just stopped thinking about it.

After he had finished stuffing the food down his throat, Samantha came back into the room and told him that she was going to drop James off at school. When she was gone Kevin turned on the TV and watched it thinking of what he was going to say to her and he fell asleep. This time he had a dream.

He saw his wife and she was pacing back and forth in their room. She had a worried look on her face and she was talking to herself. She then got on her knees and said a pray on the side of the bed. When she was finished she walked over to Kevin's closet. He couldn't see what she was doing because it started to blur out of focus. When the blur was gone there was a house that Kevin had never seen before. There was a small gnome in the yard and it had a huge smile on its face. Then there was a flower in the middle of the yard that looked like a blue rose. The house was blue and looked as if someone had painted it to match the flower. The shutters on the house were a different color blue and so was the sidewalk, but it still looked like a nice and comfortable home. While Kevin began to admirer the house it started to fade away and soon another house came into view. But Kevin knew whose house it was. His parents' or the one they used to own. No one had moved into the house after Kevin had left it and it looked ragged and worn out. Kevin saw a car drive up into the driveway and Samantha got out. She walked around to the trunk and pulled something out. Then the dream returned to Kevin's room. Samantha had just walked into the door and she had Kevin's shotgun in her hands.

Kevin woke up and thought about these things. He had two questions. One was what was Samantha doing, and the second was why was he being told all of this information. He thought that there must be something wrong with Samantha and she didn't want to worry him. Maybe she had some old boyfriend trying to blackmail her or something. Kevin was worried about her, but something made him not care as much as he should have. He was more worried about his sons.

He didn't know what he would do if she mixed up his children in this mess. He had to figure things out. Then a thought came to him. Who was telling him all of this? Could it be that woman? He couldn't understand why she would want to do something to Samantha. Was she in love with him or something? Or was there something more than she wanted or needed?

He wanted to clear his head so he could think, so he decided that he should go for a walk. He put on some clothes and walked out of his room. Keith and William were sitting in the living room waiting for the bus.

"Hey, Dad," they both said, looking and then turning back to the TV.

"Have you two seen your mother going out, without telling anyone?" asked Kevin as he sat down in the other couch.

"Not me," said Keith.

"Well," said William. "I called home once to check and see if Mom would bring me some things for a class later on in the day, but she wasn't home and I call three times. I even called her cell phone, but there was still no answer. Mom usually always answers the phone."

"How do you remember something like that?" asked Keith, trying to make William feel like a fool.

"I have a great memory, unlike you. You forget about everything, except how to play football."

"All right. That's enough," said Kevin, getting up to leave.

"Father," said William.

"Yes?"

"Why did you want to know about Mother and what she was doing?" Kevin had to think of a moment. He wasn't going to tell them the truth even though he thought they would want to know, and that they would soon find out.

"I was just wondering if she was doing some early Christmas shopping; I didn't want to get left out of all the fun. Hey, what do you two want for Christmas?"

"I want some money?" said Keith.

"I don't know yet, Father. Christmas it still sixty-six days away. I'll have to talk to you about it later."

"Okay, I'm going for as walk. I'll see you later." Then Kevin walked out of the house.

It was humid outside, but Kevin felt good. This was strange though, because he really couldn't feel much of anything and still it felt good. He started to walk down the street enjoying the view. Everything looked pleasing to him, from the birds in the trees, to the ants that were crawling on his shoes, which he usually would have killed but now he liked the sight of them. Just about everyone that lived in his neighborhood had clean cut grass and a nice looking house. He had never really paid much attention to how beautiful the world was. It was as if he was seeing through different eyes and everything had changed from horrid to magnificent. He continued to enjoy looking at the sky and the sun as he walked, but today he wanted to pay closer attention to the houses. He was looking for the one he had seen in his dream. He hoped that he could find some kind of answers there. That was the only lead he had on what was happening to him. Even though everything seemed as if it was normal, better than normal, he still couldn't ignore what was happening to him. He really didn't know who was giving him the dreams, or why. All he could assume was that the Old lady was playing some kind of game with him and he was falling for it like a fool. The truth was that he really didn't want to fight her. He didn't know why, but he wanted something from her just as bad as she wanted something from him. Maybe they could reach some kind of agreement. Kevin thought of these things as he walked and soon he came to a park.

He had many memories of this park. He tried not to walk by it too often, but he sometimes found himself there without even trying. It was as if it was a part of him and he couldn't get rid of it and there was reason for that. He had played on it as a child and his grandfather had taken him there the day he disappeared.

"Kevin, are you having fun?" asked Ron.

"Yes, Grandfather, everything is fine." Kevin was sitting on the swing and his grandfather, Ron, was sitting on the bench watching him. It was a sunny day and there were lots of kids running around. The park consisted of two slides, two swing sets, and a vast field on both sides, but to the back was a forest. Kevin had never been into the forest and was told never to go in. He had heard many stories about this forest and he was too frightened to go in and find out for himself. He thought that he would have to be as foolish as his friends to do something like that and he always saw himself smarter than them.

Kevin started to kick his legs so that he could swing. He never played much with the other kids around the park; most of them didn't even want to talk to him. He asked his grandfather if it was because he was black and he told him it was because they were people who were trapped inside of the world and Kevin had been shown the way out, and they didn't want him to leave them here to rot away. Ron had told him that one day they would see the truth and good things would happen. Kevin didn't understand it then and he still didn't. He was told over and over again that God was the key and he had tried it for a moment in time, but it just didn't work. He didn't have the courage to stick to God. This was something that he hated people to say. He felt a lot better saying that he was just the one who has the courage to leave and that he would rather be free and rot in hell than to be a servant of God.

Soon it was time for Kevin to go home and his grandfather was walking him back. They were just about to go out of the park when they ran into a squirrel. The squirrel had a broken leg and it looked as if it had a lot of internal bleeding. It could barely move and it was shaking as if it was having a break down. Ron was always known as a great man and he couldn't stand to leave such a creature on the ground just waiting to die.

"Grandfather, what's wrong with the little squirrel?"

"Well, he's dying," said Ron as calmly as he could.

"What are we going to do? We have to do something?" said Kevin, pulling on his grandfather's arms.

"I can't do much, but you and I can pray to God and ask him for help."

"Okay." They both kneeled down and started to pray to God. Soon Ron stopped and looked at Kevin with a face that was unfamiliar to Kevin.

"It seems that it's his time to go and there's nothing we can do about that."

"What do you mean? Why would something this terrible be allowed to happen?"

"God works in mysterious ways," said Ron, smiling. Kevin started to cry and he put his head against his grandfather.

"Hey, don't cry. Everything has a good side to it. I think I know what we can do."

"What is that?"

"I'll take him to the forest so he can die and be at rest. Wait here." Ron picked up the squirrel and started to walk over to the forest. Kevin just sat on the ground and cried. He couldn't believe that he had prayed with all his heart for the little squirrel to be okay and nothing had happened. He didn't understand what could be the good side to death. What else it there? He couldn't imagine anything beyond his inferior world. Kevin looked up as he was still crying. Horror started to come over him. He could not believe his eyes. His grandfather was going into the forest. He wanted to scream out to him that he shouldn't go out there alone, but then he remembered God. He was certain that God would take care of his grandfather and bring him back to him so that he could be happy. He knew in his heart that God could do everything and not even that horrid forest could stand against his might. Kevin just waited and prayed that maybe the squirrel could still come back and everything could be okay.

Soon it got dark and Kevin just sat there alone. He didn't know what to do. He wasn't sure of the way home because of the dark and he didn't want to leave his grandfather. He got up and walked around waiting, and it seemed like he had waited for forever. People had walked by and looked at him, pointing as if he was an animal at the zoo or something. Everyone that was playing at the park was gone and he was left alone. Kevin walked over to the swing to wait. He would have gone in but he was told not to go into places like that alone. So he continued to wait, still not doubting that his grandfather was going to come back and walk him home.

Soon three other people came to the park. They were doing drugs, and were looking for something dangerous to do. They looked like teenagers to Kevin, but they may have been a lot younger. Everyone looked like giants when he was little. At first they just stayed over on the other side of the park smoking and doing whatever they wanted, but then one of the boys noticed Kevin. They started to walk over to him. He was shocked with fear, but then he tried to hide behind a trash can. It was too late. They had already seen him.

"Hey, little boy. Come out from behind that trash can. We won't hurt you," said one of the boys.

"Ya, we're just wondering what you're doing out here," said another, taking a step closer. Kevin hesitated and then slowly walked out from behind the can. The light was on him and the boy saw that he was black. They were surprised because they hadn't seen any young black people around their town, and of course they weren't very fond of his kind of people.

"Your black. A nigger. What might you be doing out here?" Kevin just sat there and said nothing. He didn't know what to say. He was sure that he didn't want to let them know that he was alone, but he knew that they must have known it already because he was trembling with fright.

"So you're alone. You must belong to Mr. Ron. How come you're out here alone?" Kevin still didn't answer.

"Hey, you want to have some fun?" asked the boy to Kevin. Kevin just shook his head no.

"I think you do." The boy reached out for Kevin and grabbed his shirt. Kevin kicked him in the shin and released himself and started to run. He thought of going into the forest, but he was afraid of getting lost. The boy caught Kevin before he got too far and pushed him hard in the back making him fall to the ground.

"I didn't say you could leave," said the boy, kicking Kevin in the side. "I hate you, nigger. My dad told me that once you started to come you'd take over everything." He kicked Kevin again. "Just like my father's job. He had work for years to get that promotion and your grandfather just came and took it. I'm going to beat you until your face looks as white as mine." He then jumped on Kevin and started to hit him. The boy was stronger than him and he didn't stand much of a chance. Kevin moved his hand around the ground and found a stick. He swung it at the boy and cut him across his cheek. Kevin took this chance to run. He ran down the street even though he didn't know where he was going. He was not breathing, but he also wasn't out of breath. He felt like he could have raced anyone and have beaten them without having to run at all.

Soon he found his mother and grandmother looking for him and his grandpapa. Kevin then told them about what had happened and that grandpapa had just left and never came back out from the forest. They quickly ran home and called the police, but the search couldn't start until the next day because of the twenty-four hours missing rule. Kevin couldn't sleep that entire night. He knew something was wrong with his grandfather and that he would never see him again. He was angry with God and he blamed it all on him. He couldn't believe that God would let his grandfather, who was just like a father to him and always made him say his prayers at night, disappear without a trace. He tried to tell himself that there was still hope and that the search team could still find him, but he could no longer bring himself to believe such things. That's when he first started to hear his grandfather's words in his head. "Everything has a good side to it." That night Kevin thought that was nothing more than a myth. He also did something that he had not done in a while. He didn't say his prayers.

In the morning they all set out to look for Ron. Many of the neighbors came to help, but Kevin wouldn't talk to any of them. He hated white people and God. He would have given anything at the time to just destroy them all. There was nothing he wanted more at the time. If he had been a man, he would have stormed the town and killed everything in it. He was ready to sell his soul to Satan so that he could have the power to destroy everything. If his mother had not tried to comfort him, he might have done just that and have been even worse off than he is now. His very own life meant nothing to him and suicide was at the top of his list of things to do. Kevin hated life and everything that God had ever created.

Kevin and his grandmother stayed in that night while everyone went on looking. Kevin had wanted to help, but he was a little afraid of going out into the night. He really couldn't remember what the boys looked like other than they were white and the police weren't all that interested in his case in the first place. The only reason they were looking for Ron was because he was once a very important lawyer and his disappearance would bring up many questions. Everything has a good side, right?

Kevin stood in front of the park just staring for a few moments. He had never been back here since that day. He sometimes had nightmares of it and he just wished he had then been as strong as he was now. He would have killed those boys and shown no mercy. He would have beaten them until their skin had turned black and then he would have still killed them. Kevin's anger continued to grow and then suddenly he heard, "Go into the park!" He wasn't sure if he should listen, but something inside of him made him want to go so he did. He walked over to the swing and looked at it. He could picture himself sitting there laughing and having a good time.

"I wish I had never come here on that day," said Kevin out loud.

"It wasn't you fault," said the voice. "It was the damn white people. What makes them think that they're better?"

"They didn't do anything to my grandfather."

"Yes, but they abused you, a innocent little child."

"I might have done the same thing if there had been a white boy alone in my neighborhood. I mean when I was younger."

"Maybe you're right. Let's forget about the white people and do something else. Let's go into the forest and see what we can find." Kevin turned his head and looked at that dreadful place. He still felt a little afraid of it and as if he shouldn't go. It was as if he was a child again and all of his fears had come back. He wished that he could get over his fear, but it was impossible. This fear was to stay with him forever.

"Are you afraid? Why should you be? Come on, I want to show you something." Kevin shook his head and turned to walk away when the old lady appeared in front of him.

"I really need to show you something," she said with a frown on her face.

"How did you get here?" asked Kevin, amazed at what he was seeing.

"Don't worry about that. Come on." She grabbed his hand and started to lead him to the forest.

"What kind of game are you playing with me?" She let go of his arm and smiled as she walked into the forest. Kevin didn't know why he did it but something told him to follow her, in to the place he never wanted to enter. He was following her into a place that still frightened him. The sun was up and it didn't look very scary for now, but there were leaves on the ground covering everything and Kevin thought about the possibilities of spiders. He wasn't afraid of them, but he knew how deadly they could be and would rather have nothing to do with them than to come in contact with one. Kevin walked over lots of fallen trees that were decaying. He saw just about every kinds of insects he had ever seen right there on one of the trees. He wondered what he had to be afraid about in this place. It wasn't any different from any other forest that he had ever been in. In fact, he had seen many scarier things that this.

He walked for about five minutes and he knew he was already far enough to have dropped off a dying squirrel, so what was his grandfather doing. Something must have gone wrong, but what? Why would his grandfather have wanted to continue on father through this forest? There was no reason for that. *Could something have drawn him in by force?* thought Kevin. Was there really something evil in the forest? Kevin couldn't answer any of these questions and now he had gone too far to go back. He had to continue on and find the old woman.

Soon Kevin came to an opening. The light was shining through the gap in the trees and it almost looked like a paradise in the middle of a wasteland. There weren't any leaves on the floor and the grass was perfect. It was the greenest grass Kevin had ever seen. He didn't even know that grass could get that green. It was amazing and that's all anyone could say about it. Kevin walked out into the middle of the paradise and started to swing around in circles. He didn't know why but this place made him feel happy. He felt as if he didn't have a worry in the world. He felt as if the world wasn't such a bad place and maybe, just maybe there was a chance that God still cared for him. He felt as if everything bad thing that had ever happened to him had gone away and were taken from his soul. He wanted to stay in this place forever and never have to worry about the other things that were going on in the world. He would not have to worry about men being beheaded, or about wars going on for no reason at all. If Kevin still believed in Heaven, he would have been standing there at that very moment.

"You like it here, don't you?" said the old woman who was standing behind him. Kevin turned around and looked at the woman. She looked normal. Every other time Kevin had seen her she looked malicious and dreadfully hideous, but now she still looked old but saccharine and innocent.

"What do you want with me?" asked Kevin as he stopped turning.

"I just want to help you. I know of all of your painful memories and all of your misery. I have seen everything that the world has taken away from you. I feel all of that pain also. I can't even imagine how you manage to live with all of this inside of you each and every day. I saw your father, and what he did to your mother, and how he never did much of anything good to or for you." Kevin just sat there staring at her. She had somehow gotten into this mind; of course he knew that she had been talking to him, and that she had led him here for a reason, but he never thought that it was possible for her to get inside of his head and read his thoughts and memories. "I know everything. I know how much you love your wife. I know how much you love your children. I know how much you want them to be happy. I know you would give anything for them, and would never let anyone hurt them. I know all of your secrets; even the one that you don't want everyone else to know. You know the one you kept from your family about the real reason you left Germany." Kevin was shocked. There was no way that she could know about that. Kevin didn't even know about that anymore. He had it erased from his memory by hypnosis. He couldn't even remember going to get the hypnosis, all he remembered was that he had a note that he had written to himself, during the process, which told him it had worked.

"There's no way you could know about that. I don't even know about it. I made myself forget."

"You see, that's your downfall. If you made yourself forget that means all you did was push it into a part of your mind that you would never look into. All I had to do was uncover it."

"I don't believe you. There's no way you could know about that."

"Then I might explain it to you. Let me see. It was November third, and around nine o'clock. Your friend Fred came by and asked you to go out with him. You didn't want to go but he reminded you that you owned him a favor, and being that you always pay back your favors, you were obligated to go, right?" Kevin didn't speak, but he was starting to remember bits and pieces of that day. Kevin's head started to pound from the burst of new memories. He felt as if he was learning too much at one time and he couldn't take it.

"He took you out of town and into a city that you had never been to before. Soon you both came to a club and Fred asked you to come in with him. You told him that there was nothing for you inside of a club and if he had brought you all the way out here to just go clubbing he could just take you home right now. He told you to just calm down and come in with him." Kevin's headache grew worse. He put his hand on his head, but it didn't help any. He kept seeing Fred's face with blood on it. He couldn't remember what had happened to him and he didn't want to.

"Please...could you stop? I can't take all of this," said Kevin, holding his head trying to stop the pain.

"Oh, Kevin. If you don't toughen up there's going to be a lot more pain coming your way. I suggest you try to handle it. Now...where was I? Oh, yes the club. He somehow persuaded you into going in with him. You followed him through the club until you came to a table where many people you knew from work were sitting. They said hello and then you sat down. Fred ordered you and him some drinks and then told you his story. He told you of how he had met this man named Teufel. He told you he met him at a club and he stole his money. Fred had paid for this girl and she and some other men beat him and took his wallet. He was unconscious for a while and by time he woke up all of his money was gone. He had to go and stay with one of his friends until he got his paycheck and he could afford to take care of himself. Then he spent weeks searching for Teufel and found out that he had done the same thing to many other people and they all got together to stop him. The police had tried, but Teufel had many of them on his payroll and there was not much they would do. Fred told you that he had found out that his headquarters for the night was here at this club and they were going to have a word with him. Someone then gave you a gun from under the table." Kevin started to shake from the pain. He could now remember everything he had felt, as they got ready to go and meet Teufel. Kevin would never have gone if he hadn't been drunk. He hadn't remembered much the day after, but now everything seemed extremely clear.

"Soon you found yourself at another table that belonged to Teufel. Fred and the rest of them yelled something at him, but you were too drunk at the time to understand. Soon Teufel got up from the table and started to walk away. Fred told all of you to follow him. You walked through a door and found yourself inside of another part of the club. It was an office room and Teufel had more of his men waiting there for him. You saw all of the men and heard him tell Fred that this was his last chance and that he never wanted to see him again, and you stayed for some reason. Why, I don't know? Soon their guns started to fire and you took a shot too, didn't you? Who knows if you hit anyone. You jumped behind the first thing you could find and hid until you thought it was safe." Kevin fell to his knees. He remembered everything now and the pain was too much. His head felt like it was going to burst; like it was a volcano and it would soon erupt and destroy everything. It was something he hoped he would never have to feel again, but now it was all back imprinted into the front of his mind.

"Do I need to say the rest? No, I think you remember it all now," said the old lady, smiling.

"Why are you doing this?" said Kevin, trying to get to his feet but he fell back down.

"I just wanted you to know that I know everything about you. I didn't mean to cause you any pain, but if that's what it takes then I'll do it."

"I don't even know why you're here."

"That will come in time, but for now I haven't even talked to you about why we came here. I'll give you a minute to revive yourself."

Kevin didn't know what to think. He was frightened a little, but not as much as he should have been. This woman was crazy and he felt as if there was nothing that he could do to stop her from being here; of course he was stronger than her and he could easily have killed her, unless she really could move as fast as she did at Rachel's house. Kevin had thought that Rachel had drugged him with the pizza and that's why he saw everything that he had. Now he was starting to doubt himself. He also had a feeling of want for her. He couldn't really understand it. It felt as if she was a pretty girl and he wanted to talk to her, but it wasn't exactly the same. He knew that something bad would happen if he allowed her to continue talking to him, but something made him. Something made him want to speak with her, and he wondered what she could offer to him.

"Are you alright now?" she asked as Kevin got to his feet.

"Yes, I'm fine," said Kevin, taking his hand off his head. His pain had just disappeared and he was sure that she had done it. "Did you take away my headache?"

"No, you did."

"What do you mean?"

"You'll find out. Here, let me show you something." The old woman put her hands behind her back and smiled. It was a horrible smile and it sent chills down Kevin's spine. He jumped back and almost fell. Soon she pulled something from behind her back that Kevin didn't expect to see. It was a squirrel.

"I know you remember this." She put the squirrel out in front of her. "I saw all everything that happened. You were so afraid and then you became so lonely. You couldn't trust your own father to be there for you."

"What the HELL do you know?"

"I know everything. Haven't I told you that before?" She started to walk towards Kevin. He wanted to run, but he couldn't.

"I'm a part of you now, and you and I should learn to work together.

Don't worry I won't leave you like your father did, or like your grandfather. I'm here until the end. You can trust me, Kevin, unlike your wife."

"What does that mean?" said Kevin as the old woman put her face in his.

"I am going to show you something that you need to learn how to use. Not many people get this privilege." She then placed the squirrel in Kevin's hands and she held his hands. Then she moved them so Kevin would crack the squirrel's spine. She continued to move his hands downward until blood came squirting out from the squirrel, and it got on Kevin's face. Kevin threw the squirrel on the ground and started to wipe his face.

"Oh, you don't like blood. That's something that I suggest that you get used to." She then started to walk away.

"Why did you do it?"

"Why not. Did you not want me to?"

"I don't want anything to die for no reason. There's no point to it. That's ruthless and cruel."

"And what are you going to do," she said, disappearing.

"Where'd you go?"

"I'm right here," she said in Kevin's ear. He jumped and fell onto the floor. "Why don't you just heal it?"

"How would I do that?"

"Just touch him."

"What?"

"Just touch him. Go on." Kevin thought that was the craziest thing he had ever heard, but his hand started to reach out for him. He tried to pull it back but it wouldn't come.

"What are you doing?" asked Kevin, looking at the old woman.

"Nothing, I'm standing right here, you're doing that yourself." Soon Kevin touched the squirrel and nothing happened.

"Nothing's happening."

"You have to think of it being healed and it will be." Kevin closed his eyes and pictured the squirrel alive and running around. He then felt heat go into his arm; it was like he was getting into a warm shower and he put his arm in to check if it was ready yet. Then it turned reddish brown and the squirrel started to shake. It flopped around like a fish or something and then it just stopped. Kevin got to his feet and looked at his hand. It had turned back to normal but was still shaking. Soon the squirrel got to its feet and ran off into a tree. Kevin was in shock. He couldn't explain the feeling he had. It was greater than anything he had ever felt before. He felt happy, strong, and confident at the same time. He felt like nothing in the universe could stop him. He wanted to thank the old woman for whatever she had done, but he didn't see her anywhere.

"Hey, old lady, where did you go? Hey!" There was no answer. Kevin called out for a little while longer, but soon he gave up. He started to walk out of the forest and he was wondering where she had gone. She said all that mess about staying by his side and she was gone in five minutes, but that didn't matter to him. He had all the power he needed. There was nothing to worry about. He felt as if there was nothing that he couldn't do, and that there was no one to stop him. He continued to walk until he heard something behind him. He turned around and found nothing. He started to walk again, and he heard the sound once more. He turned around again, and still found nothing. He turned around to start walking and he saw a wolf. It was a black one and looked irate and ravenous. It had foam dripping down from its mouth and was growling at Kevin. He just stood there and moved slowly to the side of it, but it jumped in the way.

"You won't just walk around him," said the old woman who was sitting up in a tree. "This is one of my old friends. I've ordered him to kill you."

"Why did you do that?"

"To see what you would do. Now it's time to find out." The old woman pointed at Kevin and the wolf attacked. Kevin managed to move out of the way, and he started to run through the woods. "You won't get far!" yelled the old lady as Kevin ran off with the wolf close behind him. He was trying to get his arm to work again, but he felt nothing. *Think about death,* thought Kevin. He tried but he was thinking too much about running and staying alive. He knew that this wasn't an ordinary animal. Suddenly, he tripped on a stick and fell down on his face. The wolf quickly jumped on his back and started to bite him. He ripped his shirt and scratched at his back. Kevin had braced himself for the pain, but he felt nothing. He thought at first that he must have been dead already and now he was somewhere else as his body remained behind to be tortured, but then he move and threw the wolf off of him. The wolf quickly got to its feet and tried to bite Kevin's neck as he got up, but Kevin moved his neck just in time. The wolf went past him and hit his head into the tree that was in front of Kevin. Kevin heard a loud "crack" and then saw blood on the tree. He got to his feet and dusted himself off.

"I didn't even have to use my hand to kill that one. You should have tried harder, old woman," said Kevin, smiling even though he didn't know what was so funny.

"Do you really think he's dead?" said the woman. She was standing right next to Kevin with a smile on her face. She looked as hideous as ever.

"What do you mean? Don't you see the blood…?" Kevin turned to point at the tree, but there was nothing there; the blood and the wolf were gone. "What happened to it?"

"To what, Kevin? I don't remember you doing much of anything. Hey, you better watch your leg."

"What?" said Kevin as the wolf came up and bit his leg. He quickly shook him off and turned to face him. The wolf jumped up into Kevin's chest and tried to bite him. Kevin grabbed the sides of his mouth and held him back. The wolf was kicking its legs to free itself but it did nothing to Kevin. Kevin forced his hand outward and broke the wolf's jaw. Blood came out of its mouth and hit Kevin in the face. Kevin dropped the wolf and tried to wipe his face. As he did this, the wolf got to its feet and moved behind Kevin. Then it charged and knocked Kevin in the air. He came down hard on his back and got the wind knocked out of him. Then the wolf moved on top of him and pinned him down.

"You're going to have to do better than that," said the old woman. She was petting the wolf and smiling. "You're going to have to learn more about that hand if you're going to use it right. You could have killed my pet easily if you had known how." The woman then slapped the wolf and it disappeared. Kevin just lay on the ground for a moment thinking about what was happening and he came to the conclusion that he did not have a clue about what was going on.

"What is in my hand?" asked Kevin, getting to his feet.

"It's a gift that I wanted you to have. You'll find it useful."

"For what?"

"Doing whatever you want. For covering up Rachael's death."

"I didn't do it."

"Yes, I know but soon the police will find your prints and they'll come for you."

"Did you kill her?"

"Does it matter?"

"WHAT IS THE POINT OF ALL OF THIS?" yelled Kevin with all the energy he could muster.

"What do you mean?"

"I mean everything you have done to me. I'm never hungry, I can not feel pain, I heal faster than anyone could possible heal, I hate my wife, and every time I go to sleep I have some kind of weird dream."

"I don't know what you are talking about. I just wanted you to have this gift. I think you'll use it well."

"For what?"

"Everything." Then she was gone.

"Where did you go?" Kevin looked around for a while, but he found nothing. He did not want to stop looking but he had many things to think about. Soon he started to walk out of the wood. He was confused. He didn't understand why she had given him the gift in the first place or what he was supposed to use it for. His shirt was ripped and he looked at his back to see if there were any scratches, but he could not see any. It didn't make sense to him how the wolf had bitten him and he felt nothing, but then the wolf knocked him down and he was out of breath. How was that possible? It wasn't in the world Kevin lived in, but now he was starting to question his life. He could no longer believe the very things that he used to keep himself from going insane. Everything seemed wrong to him, and he didn't know how to control it. Now he was worried about the power he possessed. It had only been a few minutes ago when he had felt unstoppable and now he was terrified.

Soon he came out from the forest and he quickly tried to get home. People were looking at him like he was crazy. They couldn't believe that he had on a shirt like that and was running. One man said that they should call the police because he probably raped someone. Everyone who heard him laughed, except for Kevin. He got angry. He couldn't believe that after all this time that he had lived here in peace with all of them they still treated him as if he was nothing but a raping, thrash talking, stealing black man. He had done many things for that man in particular. When no one wanted to help him Kevin came by and gave him a hand. He did this for him and the other people in the neighborhood that he would usually never have done to help anyone, but they were just using him because he was black. *Someday there going to have to pay*, thought Kevin as he walked into his house.

It was three o'clock and all of the kids were gone. Kevin hoped he wouldn't find Samantha and he was glad when he didn't. He figured that she was out doing some shopping or something. He quickly took of his shirt and threw it into the trash. Then he went and took a shower. He still couldn't feel the water and he wasn't dirty, but it helped to calm his nerves. He remembered the old lady saying that the police were going to find his fingerprints and come and get him. If that happened he couldn't lie to them anymore and then they would think that he killed that woman and that everything he said from now on would be considered a lie. Kevin thought about going back to the house, but he knew that there was nothing he could do now. They surely must have already found some prints and they would just look up his records and find a match.

He got out of the shower and walked to his room. He was starting to feel the headache again and he lay down to rest. He still didn't know what the old woman wanted, but he felt almost obligated to wait until she told him. He had a strong eagerness to allow her to do what she wished. He felt as if she could help him to do what ever he wanted, but what did he want? He closed his eyes and pictured something horrible that he knew he would never do, but still he wanted it to happen.

Soon Kevin fell asleep. He found himself inside of the white space again. It looked the same, but felt a little different. He didn't know exactly what it was, but it seemed to be tranquil and peaceful though it was still as empty as it was before. Kevin started to wonder what this place was and why he had come here. He had never dreamed of this before the old lady came and he couldn't use his mind to try to create anything. As he pondered over this a road appeared under his feet. He reached down and touched it to see if it was real and it was. It felt just like any other road Kevin had ever touched. It was warm as if the sun had been extremely hot that day and had been shining on it for hours. Kevin looked up into the sky, but he didn't see a sun at first. Then one appeared from out of nowhere. Kevin had to quickly cover his eyes so he wouldn't go blind. The rays from the sun were a lot stronger than those of the sun in the real world, but they soon cooled down.

Kevin took off the jacket he had on and threw it to the side. He didn't know why he had had it on. He didn't even own a jacket that looked like that. It was baby blue in color and looked more like a cloak than a jacket. It was silky feeling, but Kevin couldn't tell if it was real or not. He had some pants on that looked the same as the jacket and some matching shoes. He figured that it was just some dream clothes that went along with this weird place. Why? He did not know but was determined to try to find out.

Kevin started to walk down the road. He went for miles and didn't notice any change in anything. It seemed to him that he had been in the same spot the whole time. The sun hadn't moved and the temperature was still the same. Kevin walked on this road for what seemed like hours and finally he saw something off in the distance. He couldn't tell what it was, but he knew something was there. He started to run so he could get there faster, and it got bigger and bigger as he got closer to it. Soon he saw that it was a cabin house. It had white flowers everywhere in the yard and there was smoke coming out of the chimney, but it didn't go anywhere. It would go about two feet into the air and then just disappeared. The logs on the outside of the cabin were made of redwood and shined like they had just been polished.

The grass was cut evenly around the entire yard and looked extremely fresh. The last thing Kevin noticed about the house was that there was a pond in the back yard.

Kevin walked up to the front of the house and stopped to look at it. It was a beautiful house that looked as if someone really cared for it and wanted people to admirer it. The walkway looked very nice. It was also made of redwood and was placed in a curve-like structure. The front door looked as if it was made of the same wood, but it was black. There was a bird on top of the house. It just sat there and Kevin thought it was a statue with very good details. He started to walk up the walkway and he could feel the softness of the wood even though he had shoes on. Kevin could not help but admire how the grass was higher than the walkway, but none of it touched the walkway. Everything in this house was perfectly groomed and fixed. *Someone would have to come out here every day and cut to keep it looking like this all of the time*, thought Kevin, as he grew closer to the door.

Kevin knocked on the door three times, but no one answered. He screamed to ask if anyone was home, but once again he didn't get an answer. He was determined to get into the house and he walked around to look for a window. He hadn't noticed any before, but he thought that was just because he hadn't looked. When he didn't find one he went back to the front door and tried to knock one more time. When there wasn't an answer he got mad and told himself that he would find a way into the house. Kevin looked down and saw that there wasn't a doorknob and he was sure that there had been one before. He pushed on the door and it slowly budged. It was heavy and felt too heavy for just a door. The door was very skinny and some how it weighed a ton. It took Kevin about two minutes to open it.

Inside it was dark and Kevin could not see much of anything except for a small candle. He walked over to it and tripped on something. He couldn't see what it was but it felt like a table. He got to his feet and moved over to the candle again. This time he used his hands to try to feel around, but he didn't run into anything else. Once he got the candle he walked back to where he had fallen and looked for what he had tripped on. It was at table and Kevin had seen it the last time he had been here. He was sure that it was the same table and he even saw the cup that had hit him in the face when he woke up. He wondered how this house had gotten here. There wasn't any wood anywhere inside of this place and there weren't any tools that whoever did this could have used. Then the question why came into Kevin's head again. Why would anyone do all of this? Kevin continued on through the house to searching for the answer.

The next room he entered was the kitchen. There was another candle in the room, but it was still dark. There was a table that was set as if someone was going to eat on it soon and that was the first thing Kevin found that gave off the idea that someone was here. Kevin looked around for a stove, but only found pots and pans that were on the floor. He looked inside of one of them and saw it was rusty and had something rotten in it. Kevin quickly pulled his head back. He didn't want to look again, but he had to see it. He looked one more time just to make sure and found his theory to be correct. The pot was filled with rotting meat. It looked as if it had been there for a long time, but there was one thing wrong with it. This meat smelled worse than anything Kevin had ever smelled, but there were not any bugs anywhere. Why would they not be there?

He walked away from the pot and looked around the rest of the room. He couldn't find a sink, or any chairs for the table, or even any drawer that the pots might have gone in. There also wasn't anything in the room to cook on. There wasn't anywhere someone could have started a fire without burning the house down with it. Kevin hadn't seen anything outside that they might have used and where would they get food in the first place? The only things around here to eat were the plants in the yard. The stuff in the pot had looked green, but Kevin was almost a hundred percent sure that it was meat. The only thing wrong with that, was that there was not anywhere around for anyone to get any kind of meat.

Once he got to the door something told him to look around one more time and he did. He looked from the left to the right and found something that wasn't there before. There was some kind of box that had appeared in the center of the room. Kevin walked over to it and touched the top. It was very cold and Kevin thought he was touching ice instead of a box. Kevin took his hand back as fast as he could and it stayed cold even after he had let go. Now his hand felt even colder than the box and soon it started to tremble. He put it next to the candle and waited for it to warm up. Then he put the candle on the box and he could hear the ice crack and start to melt. Soon liquid started to come out from the box and Kevin touched it to see if it had cooled off and then he opened it. All he found was liquid. He figured that he must have melted all of the ice and now it was water. He was closing the box when something made his candle fall in. He didn't know what but it just slipped out of his hand and fell in. Kevin quickly reached in and tried to grab the candle, but he couldn't find it. The liquid that he was moving through was thick and Kevin lost the thought of it still being water. He desperately wanted to get his hand out of the liquid, and then he thought he would just get the other candle. He got up and started to walk over to the candle, but slipped and fell on his back. He felt light come into the house.

Kevin quickly got up and out of the liquid and now that he could see the color he was sure that it was blood. He looked around for a light switch or anyone that might have came into the room and turned on the lights but he saw nothing. There were no light bulbs on the ceiling and no holes or anything for light to penetrate through. Kevin walked out of the room as fast as he could and found that the rest of the house also had light in it. Kevin saw that there was a wooden chair in the first room now and there was a quilt on it. He picked up the quilt and used it to wipe the blood off of his arms. Then he sat down in the chair to catch his breath. He wasn't afraid of blood or anything, but he just didn't like the sight of it. He was sure it was because he had seen so much of it when he was young. He had seen more blood in his own household than he had when he was in war.

Kevin got to his feet and walked back to the room to make sure that he saw what he had. It was still there but the box was red now and the blood was leaking out onto the floor. It was going everywhere and it seemed to have no end. It was like there was a pump or something that kept the blood coming. Kevin closed the door to the kitchen and put the quilt down by the bottom to keep the blood in, but soon it came through the quilt and was going into the other rooms. It was as if the blood had a mind of its own, or as if it had some kind of mission to achieve. Kevin couldn't stop the blood any longer and he was going to leave the house, but the blood froze. All of it just stopped coming. Then a line came out of the blood and went up the hall. Kevin knew that he shouldn't have followed it but he couldn't help himself.

Kevin followed it up through the hall and passed all of the other rooms. Soon it brought him to a white door. It had a little shine to it and it was kind of hard to look at. There, the blood went up the door and turned into a face. It didn't look like anyone Kevin knew, but just an ordinary face. At first it was just still, but it made a frown, as Kevin got closer to it. He didn't know why he was doing it. He was almost sure that he shouldn't have, but something inside of him wanted it. Kevin didn't know why but he kissed the face and it didn't even matter to him that it was blood. It was a passionate kiss and Kevin put all of his heart and soul into it. He wanted that kiss more than anything, even more than he wanted Samantha, or his children, or another chance to play football. That kiss meant the world to him and he would have given anything for it.

After he finished kissing the blood face, it disappeared into the door. Kevin felt a feeling of relief come over him. He felt as if a huge burden had been lifted off of his shoulders and now he had nothing to worry about. He could live life without a care and do whatever he wanted. All he had to do was give in to the presence that surrounded him. It came from a hole that appeared in the door. Kevin reached out for it as if he was drunk and couldn't control himself. It felt warm and Kevin quickly breathed in as much of it as he could. He felt like he was getting high on some kind of drug. Like he was floating in space with no one around to bother him. Like he was the center of the universe and everything evolved around him.

Soon the presence lifted him into the air. He didn't try to fight it and he didn't want to. He was willing to take whatever it was going to offer if it would guarantee him the feeling he felt now for as long as he wanted it. Kevin's life didn't even matter to him now. He didn't want to return to the real world and even if this was fake it was real enough for him to enjoy and that's all that mattered. The presence continued to lift Kevin up and increase in pleasure. It wanted to mutilate Kevin so that he would do whatever he was told and it seemed to be working. Kevin knew deep down that giving into this force, or this presence, was going to cause dreadful and disturbing thing to happen to certain citizens, but at the time that didn't matter. Nothing mattered to him at all. He just wanted to lose himself in the moment and worry about the rest later.

Soon the presence put him back down and went back into the wall. Kevin tried to keep it from leaving, but he couldn't. Kevin beat on the door furiously and when it wouldn't budge he cried with his head on the floor. They were loud cries, like a baby who wanted its bottle. He banged his hand on the floor and screamed for it to come back to him. The presence didn't come back but a voice came to him.

"Why are you crying?" asked the voice.

"The greatest feeling that I can imagine just left me. I can't bear living without it after experiencing it," said Kevin as he continued to bang on the floor.

"What would you do for the feeling?" Kevin lifted his head, but he didn't say anything.

"What would you do?" asked the voice with more persistence.

"Anything," said Kevin quietly.

"WHAT?"

"Anything you want from me. All you have to do is ask." Kevin got to his feet. "I'll do anything for the feeling and I won't let anything stop me."

"What did you say?"

"I said that I'd do anything, anything you want."

"I always thought you were a family man. What about them?"

"They don't matter anymore."

"That's what I hoped you say." Then the voice left. Everything grew silent and Kevin just sat on the ground looking for some kind of sign. Then a word of blood appeared on the door and Kevin quickly got up to read it. *Push*. That's what was on the door. Kevin put his hands on the door and pushed lightly. It didn't budge. Kevin tried it again, harder this time, but still it wouldn't move. Then another word appeared on the door. *Harder* was the word and Kevin did as he was told. Still nothing happened and the door still wouldn't move. Kevin couldn't even feel the slightest change in the door. Soon the wood started to repeat itself over and over again. *Harder, harder, harder, harder* and Kevin continued to push harder and harder, but nothing happened. Soon Kevin couldn't push any more and he fainted hitting his head on the door. Kevin lay on the ground unmoving, but some unknown strength made him continue on even though he knew he wouldn't achieve anything. He grew angry and he started to punch the door and hit the words that continued to appear on it. He couldn't feel any of the pain so there was nothing stopping him from punching through the door. It made him worry for a moment because earlier he could feel all kinds of things, but now he felt nothing. Soon the worrying left and all that remained was the chance of getting through the door and getting to the presence.

Kevin punched for hours, but he still accomplished nothing. There wasn't even a bend in the door. Kevin didn't know what to do and he knew he couldn't do much of anything so he laid his head against the door and cried. A word appeared as he did this and he jumped back and wiped the blood from his head. Then the word came back and Kevin was shocked. *Time,* what did that mean? Nothing to Kevin. He couldn't understand what that meant. He was fed up with waiting and he punched the door with all the strength he could muster. He felt his hand go through and he was relieved that he had finally broken the door. He felt a great joy spread through his bones and he couldn't wait until he got to the other side. He pulled his arm back so he could look through the hole, but he couldn't move it. He pulled and pulled, but it didn't budge. Then he looked to find his arm stuck in a hole. It was a black hole and it slowly sucked Kevin into it. Kevin couldn't fight it and he didn't want to in hope that it might take him to the other side. Once Kevin's face got closer to the door the hole stopped pulling him. Then a big blob of blood appeared above the hole. It was in a circle form and grew outwards towards Kevin. Kevin couldn't move away from it and he hoped that it was going to help him, not fight him. He was wrong. Once the blob got to his face it turned into a fist and hit him in the face. It only took one hit to knock Kevin out.

Kevin woke up in his bed with Samantha next to him. She was asleep and Kevin had slept through the day. He got to his feet and checked his head to see if he was okay, and he was. He wasn't sure of where he had gone or what he had wanted, but he knew that he had to find a way to get it. Now, that he was back in the real world he didn't think that he would give up his family for it, but he would do just about anything else. Kevin didn't want to be in the room with Samantha. He still felt pain from just being around her, but now it was kind of numb. He had to get out of the room so he went outside and sat down in a chair. He had always gone out and looked at the stars at night when he was in Germany, but it wasn't the same in Texas. He had to think of a way out of everything he was going through. He knew that he had seen worse times than this, but something just kept telling him that it was going to get worse. Although he knew this, he didn't want to worry about it now. All he wanted to do was sit out in the night and look up at the stars. He knew it was cold because of the light fog that was in the air, but he couldn't feel it at all. He sat out there until Samantha came out in the morning worried about him. She had been speaking to him for a few minutes before Kevin noticed her.

"Kevin, what's wrong with you?" asked Samantha with a slightly frightened tone.

"What? Ow, hey, Samantha," said Kevin, a little shocked to find her outside with him. He looked at her with a plain expression. There wasn't even the smallest sight of emotion in his face. Samantha almost jumped back when she saw him. She had never seen his face like that before. He always had some kind of feeling that would show up in his face and revealed how he was really feeling.

"Kevin, your face...I've never seen you look this way before," said Samantha, sitting down next to him.

"I don't know what you mean," said Kevin, trying to force a smile, but he couldn't keep it for long.

"Are you okay?" asked Samantha as she reached for Kevin's face. He tried to move with all of his strength but he couldn't. As her hand got closer to his face some of his feeling started to come back, but it wasn't the kind of feeling that anyone wanted to savor. It was a feeling of utmost disgust, and Kevin felt himself starting to vomit. Samantha's hand got about an inch from his face and all of the feeling that had been lost to him returned immediately. He felt as if his skin was going to burn off. His flesh felt as if someone had placed an iron on it and then somehow placed hot coals through his ears and into his head.

Before Samantha's hand touched him, Kevin quickly moved and vomited. Samantha jumped back and screamed. Blood was spilling everywhere from out of Kevin's mouth. There was enough blood to make at least four of five trips to the Red Cross. Kevin had his feelings back, but the loss of all that blood didn't even make him quiver. He felt as if he could have vomited for hours and not have felt any different. Samantha was shocked and couldn't do anything, but stand there. She was almost certain that Kevin was going to die and she didn't know what she would tell the police when they asked her what had happened. She knew that they would assume that she had something to do with it and try to blame this whole thing on her. She was sure that this time there was no way out.

Kevin was starting to feel less pain from Samantha as she started to leave him. Once it was entirely gone Kevin closed his mouth and got to his feet. Samantha turned around and saw him. She was relieved.

"Are you okay?" asked Samantha as she tried to reach for him again, but Kevin quickly moved away.

"Yes, I'm fine. Just be glad all the blood is in the grass and not on the porch." Kevin smiled at Samantha even though he disgusted her and wanted nothing more to do with her. He still didn't know why he wanted to be rid of her, but he was sure that he should find out.

"I'm going to go and call the doctor," said Samantha as she walked towards that house.

"No, you don't need to."

"What do you mean? You just threw up about a gallon of blood and you don't want me to call the doctor. You know Doctor Smith will personally come here to see you."

"Yes, but I don't want to bother him."

"Why not?"

"Because I'm fine." He smiled again and Samantha saw that his facial expressions had return to normal.

"You do look a lot better. Are you sure?"

"Yes, I think my body just had to get rid of some bad blood or something."

"I've never seen anyone do anything like that to get rid of some blood."

"Me neither, but I'm fine now and that's all that matters."

"Okay, whatever you think is best, but I'm going to call and check in on you every hour."

"Where are you going?"

"I promised that I would help out at the church today. Would you rather have me stay home with you?"

"No, you should go. I'll be fine." Kevin felt deep down that everything that she had just told him was a lie. He couldn't explain it but that's how he felt. Samantha turned around and walked into the house, but looked back and asked Kevin if he was okay one last time. He answered yes and continued to look at her until she was gone. He just could not understand how his wife had become his worst enemy.

Kevin then just stood outside for a moment and looked around. He could tell from the sun that it was around noon and he had wasted the day away without even noticing it. Then he started to walk back towards the house. As he walked through the door, he heard something behind his back. It was the old lady. She looked old and nasty this time and had on ripped clothes that were covered in dirt. She smiled at Kevin and he quickly noticed that she only had three teeth in her mouth and all of them were rotten. Her skin looked as if she had taken it off and wasted it in mud then waited for it to dry before she put it back on. Her eyes were twice as menacing as he had noticed them to be and they were entirely black. Kevin didn't know why, but something told him to walk back outside and talk to her. Kevin had a huge back yard and he stopped in the middle of it. The old woman was standing in front of a tree that was along the outer edge of the yard.

"What are you doing here?" asked Kevin. The old woman just stood there and smiled at him not saying a word.

"WHAT THE HELL DO YOU WANT?" The old woman put her finger on her lips and smiled again.

"You should quiet down," she said as she started to walk closer to Kevin. He took a few steps back, but then he gathered some courage and asked her again.

"What do you want with me? I need to know."

"In time you will, but tell me something."

"What?"

"Do you believe her?"

"Believe who?"

"Your wife, Samantha. Do you believe a word of anything she told you?"

"How do you know about that?"

"Don't you remember that I know everything about you? I know you don't believe her. I can help you."

"I don't need your help." Kevin started to walk away, but the old woman appeared right in front of him and stopped him.

"What do you mean? We're partners in this?"

"Partners in what?"

"You know exactly what I'm talking about."

"No I don't." Kevin was confused. He was sure that she had never told him anything about what she was planning or about why or what she wanted from him. There was nothing he could recall that would help him to solve this problem. He wanted to just hit her in the face and run away, but something inside of him told him to stay.

"Kevin, you had better wake up and watch what's happening."

"Yes, you might be right. I will watch." Kevin knew he must have gone insane and now he was talking to this old woman whom he didn't even now the name of. There wasn't anything that he could have done that was worse than this. He was just giving in to the forces inside that would lead him into nothingness and soon there would be nothing that he could do about it.

The old woman nodded her head and stepped to the side of Kevin, with a smile that looked almost happy. Kevin nodded at her also and then he started to walk towards the house. He couldn't wait to get inside and be rid of that horrible woman whom he didn't know anything about. He got to the door and the woman called his name. He turned around and saw her standing right behind him holding an ax. He couldn't move as the weapon came towards his face and sliced through his skin. It went from the left side of his face diagonally to the right and was about an inch or so deep. The cut left a small part of Kevin's left eye uncovered. After the first cut Kevin put his hand in front of him and tried to shield himself. The old woman just cut his hand and then cut his face again. Those cuts were just as deep, but felt twice as painful. Kevin couldn't fight her and he tried to back away, but he tripped and fell back on his head.

He quickly got to his feet and saw that everything that happened wasn't real. There wasn't any blood and there weren't any cuts on his hands. His face was fine and everything was just like it was before everything happened. Samantha had changed clothes and walked up behind Kevin and scared him.

"I'm sorry. I didn't mean to frighten you," said Samantha as she grabbed her purse from off of the table.

"It's okay. I was just sitting here—"

Samantha cut him off before he could finish was he was saying. "I just wanted you to know that I was leaving and if you need me I'll have my cell phone. I should be home around six, but you never know how things are going to turn out." Then she left the room. Kevin, though he didn't want to talk to her, was shocked at how she had treated him. She really didn't even pay any kind of attention to him and that wasn't like her. He thought about following her but he decided to just leave it alone for now. He walked to his room and jumped on the bed. He hadn't even done much of anything this whole day and was already ready for it to be over. He noticed that he still had the same clothes on from the other day and he went to change his clothes. Then he came back to his bed and found the old woman sitting there smiling.

He didn't have much time to say anything, because she reached up and pulled him down to the bed. Then she got on top of him and kissed him. It was a passionate kiss and Kevin felt at peace as she did this. Though she was still ugly and nasty-looking Kevin couldn't help but go along with the kiss. Kevin then started to feel some of the presence that had driven him mad only a few hours ago. He felt as if he could have fallen in love with this horrible and hideous monster at that very moment. He started to feel on the old woman and she didn't seem to resist; in fact, the presence grew stronger and Kevin wanted her more than ever. He wanted to strip from his clothing and make love to her at that very moment. He knew that if he was in his right mind he would have never wanted to do something so obscene, but at the moment it didn't matter. All of the emotion he had felt as he tried to break down that door and all of the things he said he would have given up had come back to him and now he was sure that it was what he really wanted. He couldn't imagine himself living without it.

As Kevin tried to feel more on the old hag, she grabbed his hands and removed herself from him. Then she stood at the end of the bed and smiled. Kevin sat up on the bed and looked back at her. She looked hideous, but made him feel better than any other woman ever had and they hadn't even had sex yet.

"What's wrong?" asked Kevin, taking off his shirt.

"Nothing, are you sure this is what you want?" asked the old lady, smiling.

"Yes, I know this is what I want."

"Once we do this you can't go back. You'll belong to me and only me."

"I don't care. I need you." The woman didn't say anything; she just smiled. Kevin was eager to get her into bed with him. Samantha crossed his mind but she didn't mean much of anything anymore. Nothing did. Kevin didn't care about the war, or about his family, or about Rachael and her death. All he wanted was to be with this horrible, nasty, dirt old woman so he could make love to her. It didn't matter what would happen afterwards. If Samantha left him then he would just live without her; he thought this was funny because only a week ago he couldn't even imagine living without her and now she meant nothing at all; he couldn't even stand her touch and did not want to be around her.

"Come get into the bed with me?" said Kevin, reaching out for her. She took his hand, but wouldn't let him pull her to the bed.

"Come on, what's wrong? Why won't you come?" Kevin grew more and more desperate every minute and he couldn't wait much longer; he told himself that he would rape her if he had to. Nothing was going to keep him from the great sensation that she granted him. Nothing.

"Please get into the bed," said Kevin, pulling her harder, but she wouldn't move. Kevin had to get her into the bed and he used all of his strength to try to pull her, but she didn't even move. Soon she moved her hand and Kevin got flung back into the bed.

"Are you done?" asked the old woman, laughing at Kevin.

"Why are you doing this to me?" said Kevin, taking deep breaths.

"Doing what?"

"Playing games with me. You put this feeling inside of me and now you won't give it to me. Are you trying to make me suffer?"

"Only if I have to. Get up and put back on your shirt." Kevin didn't move. He couldn't believe that she would do something to him like that. She didn't even look good. He was willing to give up his entire life for just one chance to have sex with her, and she didn't even take him seriously.

"Hurry up and come meet me at the door." Then she walked out of the room and left Kevin alone. He would have been furious but he couldn't. It was like he had fallen in love with her instantly and there was nothing he could do to break this unknown spell. He put back on his shirt and then he walked to the front door to meet the old woman. She was standing at the door waiting for him. She had changed clothes and looked almost pleasant. She wore some old looking clothes that looked like those from the eighteenth century. They looked very expensive and she had on a necklace that shined brightly. Kevin was amazed at how clothes could change her from a monster into a beauty queen.

"What took you so long?" she asked, smiling like always.

"I'm sorry I…"

"It doesn't matter. Come on, I want to take you somewhere."

"Okay." Kevin followed her outside. The sun was high in the calm sky and it felt peaceful. The old woman walked over to Kevin's truck and pulled the keys out of her pocket.

"How did you get those?" asked Kevin as he got into the passenger's seat.

"I saw them on the table, does it really matter?" she said with an attitude.

"You don't need all of the attitude." Kevin noticed that she wasn't as pleasant as she usually was. She had changed, and he couldn't help but feel that she was evil. Not like a demon or anything, but worse. He felt almost scared to sit next to her. She still had her smile, but it also had changed into something worse.

"So where are we going?" asked Kevin as they took off down the street.

"You'll know when we get there." She turned and smiled at Kevin, but he could tell that it wasn't the same as before. They drove down the road and to the right. Kevin had never gone down this road and he had no idea of where they were going. They drove through some woods and soon they came to another neighborhood. It looked familiar to Kevin, but he could not think of why. He was sure that he had never been here before and that there was no reason that he should remember anything about it. He started to feel as if something very bad was about to happen and that he was going to be the cause of it whether he wanted to or not.

There were many people playing in the streets and the old lady stopped each time one of the children walked by. She never wanted to, but Kevin would scream for her to stop and she would smile as she put on the brakes.

"Why do you care about them? What have they ever done for you?" she asked Kevin.

"They've done nothing for me, but they are only children. I don't want them to die for no reason." Kevin had always loved children, but he had never really talked to anyone about it. He was not a pedophile or anything, but he just loved children. He would have loved to work at a daycare center or something like that, but while he was growing up he was taught that only a punk would do something like that.

"You know, I know how much you care about children. Why is that?" asked the old lady, looking Kevin in the face.

"I don't know. That's just something I always had. I can't help it. Why shouldn't I love children?" asked Kevin, kind of scared to be talking about his emotions.

"Why don't you feel that way about all people?"

"What do you mean?"

"You could care less if a man walked out in front of this truck and got hit. You wouldn't even mind if I drove off and left whomever it was there alone and hurt. Why do you care about children, but not about adults? Aren't they both human and the same in some sense?" Kevin was quiet for a moment. He was thinking about his father and all of the adults that had done him wrong. To him once people transformed from children to adults they weren't human anymore. They were no longer trustworthy and would just go about doing what they want and as they please. They would fight in wars, run from wars, fight for their lives from the people who were fighting in the war, or just sit back and enjoy the war and continue to live as if nothing was happening. They would not worry about the innocent people who were dying for no reason and would never have a chance to live their life for the very things the American Constitution stands for; liberty, peace, the pursuit of happiness, righteousness, a pleasant life, to be equal with the people whom surround you. What happened to all of that? Kevin had never seen anything that showed him that any of that was true.

"I don't know," said Kevin as he took in a deep breath. He didn't see the old lady as she turned her head and smile. She could feel Kevin hatred towards the mankind and that's exactly what she wanted to get out of him.

"I feel so sorry, Kevin. I didn't mean to cause you any pain. I was just curious."

"It's okay. I guess I shouldn't blame everyone for what happened to me."

"And why not? Not a single person tried to help you."

"They didn't know."

"Would they have cared it they had? I don't think so. I say that it's their entire fault. They should all be punished."

"How can you be that cruel?"

"What do you mean? How am I being cruel? What about your brother? Was it cruel for that man to kill him and not even go to jail for it? He just walked away like he hadn't done a thing. What do you think about that?" The mention of Kevin's brother made him angry beyond belief. He had tried his best not to think about what had happened. This was something he never wanted to remember, but he couldn't have hypnosis because he would have to forget his brother entirely. That was something he never wanted to happen though there were memories that he wanted to forget he couldn't forget everything. The thing that Kevin hated the most was that even though the man had been drinking and was found drunk when he killed his brother, there was still nothing that was going to put him in jail.

"Did Louis have to die like that? Who do you think is to blame? I'd say the world." Kevin was shocked and confused. He knew that everything that she was saying was exactly what he wanted. He didn't care about any of the people or what would happen. He had held back all of his misery and he wanted someone or everyone to pay for it. He had never had the power or the chance to make a change and now that he could he wasn't sure what he would do. The only thing that had kept him from doing anything before was the thought of ruining his life and never seeing his family, but right now that didn't matter. His children and his wife seemed to just drain out from his brain as if they had never existed. They meant nothing to him any more.

"Where are you going with this?" asked Kevin, regaining his composure.

"I only want you to know that I do really want the best for you. I only want to help you get back at the world that has punished you so and done nothing to help. Is there anything wrong with that? I only want to help."

"What's in it for you?"

"Nothing, I just want you happy."

"And why do you want that?" The old lady was shocked. She hadn't expected Kevin to say that. He had somehow used his emotions to block her from reading his mind. That showed her that she still had a lot of work to do.

"Because I have seen all there is to see about you. You can hide nothing from me and I know you as well as you know yourself. I'm almost a clone of you and I want you to be happy. I can't sit back and allow you to be miserable when I know what the cause of it is."

"I still don't understand."

"There is time for that later. We're here." Kevin looked out of the window and saw nothing, but a dead end sign. There weren't any houses around and all he saw was woods.

"What do you mean? I don't see anything, but woods."

"We have to walk from here," she said as she got out of the car. "Come on." She started to walk back down the road that they had just driven down. Kevin quickly got out of the car and followed her. He didn't know where he was and he didn't want to get lost and not know how to get back home. For all he knew he could be in another state. The time had gone by quickly and the sunset was barely visible through the trees, but Kevin knew that it was late. He still didn't know what he was doing here or what she wanted, but he figured that he should just go along with it for now; *it couldn't hurt anything, right?* thought Kevin as he called out to the old lady to wait. She stopped to wait for Kevin and then they continued walking.

Soon they were in the town again. Most of the people were gone and the sidewalks were empty. Kevin and the old lady walked in silence, but she would turn and look at Kevin every now and then. Kevin felt like he was a friend of this hideous woman when he really didn't even know her. For all he knew she was leading him into a trap, and he was helping her build it. He felt almost useless and powerless just standing next to her. If she was planning something there was almost nothing Kevin could have done at time.

Soon they came to a house and the old woman stopped. Kevin almost ran into her, but he stopped before he hit her.

"What did you stop for?" asked Kevin.

"This is the place." Kevin turned and looked at the house. It was a little house that was pink in color. The grass wasn't cut and the house didn't look that attractive. Kevin couldn't believe that anyone in a nice neighborhood like this would allow his or her house to look so ugly and cheap. The roof of the house looked as if it would all just slide off at any minute. The shutters were halfway on. The door didn't even have a handle on it and anyone could walk in as they pleased.

"What am I here for? I don't know anyone that lives here." Kevin was certain that he had no business even being by this house.

"You should go inside and look around," said the old woman smiling.

"Why would I do something like that?"

"You might find something that you'll like."

"I don't think I should even touch this house."

"And why not? You have nothing to fear from this place. What could happen? I didn't bring you here so you could die. I only want the best for you, Kevin. Don't you believe me?"

"Okay…I'll go." Kevin then walked up the walkway and to the front door of the house. It was decaying and had termites and all kinds of nasty-looking bugs on it. Kevin had never liked bugs and he would do anything not to come in contact with them, but now he felt as if he didn't have a choice. He was afraid that the woman would stop him if he tried to leave, and then she might not be that nice. He had thought about trying to use his arm to destroy her, but the only time it had worked was when she was around. He was almost certain that there was nothing else he could do but walk into this death trap.

He had to force himself to touch the door, and even then he couldn't stand it. There were at least a thousand bugs on this one door and they covered it so that most of the door couldn't even be seen. Kevin eased his hand to the door and was surprised when all of them fell off as soon as he touched it. Kevin could hear the sound of their bodies hitting the ground and landing on top of the others. They looked as if something had dried them out and now they were just shells. Now there was a huge pile of dead bugs in front of Kevin and he had to walk over it. Kevin quickly did this and moved on into the house. It was just as horrible inside and Kevin felt as if he really shouldn't be there. The first room he entered was the living room and there were bugs all in the couch and along the walls. There were a couple of spiders that were trying to eat the bugs, but it looked as if they didn't stand a chance. Kevin could hear the sound of the bugs squishing, because he stepped on about five bugs every time he took a step. Blood came soaring out of the bugs and spread throughout the floor of the room. It didn't matter much because the floor was already dirty and looked stained with all kinds of liquids. Kevin moved his way through the house until he came to an unlocked room. All of the others were locked tightly, but this one was left open. *She must have planned it like this*, thought Kevin as he walked into the room.

There wasn't much in it and it looked a little better than all of the other rooms. There was a bed against the wall on the right and it was clean and nice. There were still bugs flying around and on the bed, but this room looked the best even so. There weren't any windows and that worried Kevin. He didn't know anyone who wouldn't want a window in his or her room. They must have been crazy or something to live in such a solitude place. Kevin was almost scared by the thought of being in the room of a crazy man. Kevin walked into the room and looked around. He didn't see anything worth looking at so he went to look under the bed. There were twice as many bugs under there than in the entire house. They had built some kind of kingdom and it looked as if they were eating through the wall. There was a smell that was like nothing Kevin had ever smelt before. It reminded him of burnt cheese dripped in vinegar. The smell sent shock waves through Kevin's body and he jumped back as fast as he could. He moved just in time because some of the bugs came out from under the bed and flew around the room. Kevin had seen the bugs and thought that they might have been coming for him so he moved backwards even farther and ran into the wall. The spot on the wall that Kevin backed into wasn't really a wall. Someone had made a hole in it and then coved it back up. Whoever had done this did a poor job, and Kevin went falling backwards through the hole.

It was dark and Kevin couldn't see where or what he was falling into. He reached out his hands but there was nothing for him to grab onto. He wanted to scream but he couldn't open his mouth because of the wind coming up into his face from the fall. Kevin couldn't think of anything but of what he was going to miss. He knew that if he died he would never get the chance to feel the presence that he was willing to give up everything for. He wasn't worry about what would happen to his wife or his children. He didn't care much about them at all. They were just tools to him that he had used as an excuse to live out his life without complaints. Now that he knew that there was something else for him to live for and that he didn't have to hope for things that he knew he would never get, he just wanted one thing and that was that presence.

Kevin had no idea that this whole time he had been unconscious and that the old woman was just playing games with his mind. She had planned for him to fall through the wall and he only fell a few feet. She wanted to make sure that he would do as she wanted him to and all she had to do was promise him a chance to feel happy. She really didn't need him but without him she would have to wait even longer for her plan to become true. She wanted the world and would find a way to get it. So far Kevin had fallen for every one of her plans and he seemed absolutely under her control. She was almost certain that things were going to turn out her way.

Kevin finally saw a light coming towards him and he passed through afraid of what he might find. Once he had passed he found himself lying in dirt. It was all in his mouth and as he spit it out he saw a worm go with it. He got to his feet and wiped the dirt off of his body. When he finished doing this he looked around and to see where he was. The room he was in looked like it was part of the house but whoever had started the room never finished the floor. There were just as many bugs in this room as in the rest of the house. The only good thing about this was that all of them were on the ground and they were only worms. Kevin didn't have anything against worms and he felt a little safer around them compared to other bugs.

There was a stairway at the end of the room. Kevin had thought it was peculiar because it didn't seem to go anywhere. It went straight along the ground as if Kevin was standing on the wall instead of the floor. The roof that covered them wasn't big enough for just anyone to walk through. If Kevin wanted to continue he would have to crawl on the stairs. He wasn't sure if that was a good idea, but he had nothing to lose. He couldn't reach the hole that he had fallen from and more bugs were flying through it every second. It was as if someone had ordered them to come into the room and force Kevin to make a decision. He could sit down and wait for the bugs to overthrow him or he could take a chance and go down the stairs. He felt both choices were bad ones, but he couldn't do much of anything else. He had to move quickly or he would not get the chance to choose at all.

He quickly made up his mind to go down fighting instead of just waiting. He didn't know what was at the other end of the stairs or if it would be any better than where he was now. All he cared about was getting the chance to make it out of this house and being where he could be happy. There was only one place where he knew he could do that and he didn't care about the consequences. He had spent his life in misery and he didn't feel as if he had to anymore. Kevin was certain that ultimately humans would end up killing themselves and there was nothing he could do about that. He wasn't God, he didn't even believe in God, and he knew that there was nothing he could do. If he somehow got rich and tried to give it to the poor they would become the rich and treat others just as they had been treated. It was pointless and Kevin now saw truth. There was nothing that could be done and he would have to learn to live with that, unless he moved on and lived without it. He knew that the old lady would allow him to life without a care in the world, but what would she do then? Would she take over the world and maybe kill everyone. Did it matter?

Kevin moved towards the stairs to try and make his escape. With every step he had to swat about five or so many bugs out of his face so he could see where he was going. They had almost taken over the room and Kevin didn't have much time to get out. There were bugs all over him. They were covering his clothes and his body. They began to pile on to him and soon there were so many that he could not walk. He fell to the ground and they continued to consume him. Soon he couldn't even move his hands. He had put his face into the ground so they wouldn't go into his mouth, but he had forgotten about the worm and he had a few of them in his mouth. The bugs seemed to have no end and they just keep coming. Kevin felt helpless. He couldn't move and he knew sooner or later he would run out of breath. What could he do? Even if he managed to get to his feet the bugs would only keep coming and he would never be able to take on all of them on. He was suffocating and could do nothing about it. *Everything has a good side to it,* Kevin heard this in his head as his breath left him. *How would that help me now?* thought Kevin, as he grew angry with himself. He was about to die and he had thought about the least possible thing that would have help. What was the good side about being smashed by bugs? Weak squeezable insects were about to kill a full-grown man without a fight. Kevin thought of himself as a fool to have thought of such a thing and his anger began to grow. As this happened his body began to heat up. He felt his body start to boil inside and out. Soon his body grew so hot that the bugs started to catch on fire. It started with one and then it began to grow and spread out to the others. Soon Kevin started to feel his body become free. He could move his hands and then he got to his feet. Kevin looked at the bugs and saw that almost all of them were on fire. It looked like a cloud of fire was hovering over Kevin and it started to fall. The cloud looked redder than any red Kevin had ever seen and a little transparent at the same time. Kevin could not move from under it because just looking at the cloud put him under a trace that he couldn't escape. Something seemed magical about the cloud and Kevin wanted to know what it was.

"This is beautiful," said Kevin out loud. The cloud had just taken him over and he could not reverse whatever it was doing. He put his hands in the air and he was ready to embrace the cloud, as it got closer to him. Soon he could feel his hands grow warmer and then he was inside of the cloud. His body felt relaxed and calm. This passion was taking him over and he knew it, but he didn't want it to stop. He was giving up his soul for the chance to live a life without any worries. Was there anything wrong with that? Kevin didn't think so and he was willing to give up everything. I know that's been said before, but up until now that was fake and he didn't really mean much of what he was saying. It was just a thought at the moment and now Kevin knew that he really wanted it and that he was close to having it all for himself.

The fire continued to grow in warmth and it covered Kevin entire body. Soon it lifted him off of the ground and into the air. Kevin just let it all happen and floated around feeling happy. He felt as if he could just let it all go and not have a worry in the world. What did he care about the rest of the world? They hadn't cared about him when he was down and needed help. They were too busy fighting over a pointless cause to help out anyone who really needed it. Then after the war they would all talk about it as if they had accomplished something went they really hadn't. All they had done was add to the mess that they were already in, and forgotten about all of the little people who really needed help. *What kind of fools are they?* thought Kevin. *All of their lives are pointless and will amount to nothing in the end, and why should I live in misery because of them?*

"You don't have to," said a voice to Kevin.

"What do I have to do?" asked Kevin as he closed his eyes and floated in the sky.

"First, you have to inhale all of the fire and then you have to go into the next room."

"That's all."

"For now." Then the voice left Kevin and he opened his eyes. He quickly opened his mouth and began to breathe in the smoke. It didn't have much of a taste to it, but it made him feel as if he was getting high; like he had snored pounds and pounds of cocaine into his noise all at once; like he had drunk hundreds of beer and still wanted more. It took him about thirty seconds to inhale it all and then he felt so woozy that he had to sit down for a moment to try to regain his composure. Then he got to his feet and walked over to the stairs. He knew that it was going to take all of the strength he had left to make it through this tunnel, but he was willing to do it if it would give him what he wanted. He pulled himself into the stairway the best he could and then he started to crawl through. Every time he moved forward the stair behind him would cut his knee. There wasn't any pain, but Kevin could feel the blood coming out of it as he continued on. His body began to ache after he had crawl for about an hour but he was determined to keep going. He knew that he had to make it there and it was to late to go back. *That would be twice as hard to do as going forward*, thought Kevin, making an excuse to keep going.

Soon Kevin could see a light that helped him to keep going. He wasn't sure of what he would find and it didn't matter much to him. For the time being he just wanted to make it out of this trap he was in. He would worry about the old woman once he had done that and then he would do whatever it took to get want he wanted. While he was pulling himself through he thought about how crazy he must seem to be doing all of this for something that he didn't even know how to get. He was trusting in this old woman whom he really didn't know and she might just be using him and then he would get nothing and would have wasted his time. He didn't want all of the pain he used to live with and after going through everything that he had in his life he could not bear the thought of having to go back to work and live a normal life. He thought that maybe he should try a different approach to being happy. He thought that maybe he could try to turn his life around and try to change the world before it entered the point of no return, but then he thought that the only way he could possibly do anything like that was to believe in something that he didn't. It would take God to change all of the wrong in the world and that was something that Kevin didn't have. He wasn't willing to embrace something that he had learned to live without and he figured that even with God all would be lost. *Why should I help in the first place?* thought Kevin as he crawled into the light that had taken him hours to get to.

He found himself inside of another room, but this time he wasn't alone. There was someone else in the room, but Kevin couldn't tell whom it was. The person was tied up in a chair on the other side of the room. There was blood in front of him and on the ropes that held him down. His face was covered with some kind of paper and there was blood on that also. The person's head was lying against his or her chest and there wasn't any kind of movement that showed that the person was alive. Kevin slowly walked over to the person and lifted their head. It fell right back down once Kevin let go and he was sure that whoever it was, they were dead and there was nothing he could do for them now. He wanted to take off the face covering, but he didn't want to abuse a dead person's body. From the smell Kevin could tell that it had been there for some time and it might have been mostly decayed. If it had been, he wouldn't be able to tell who it was anyways and it would be pointless to take the covering off. He stood there for a moment longer, but then decided that it would be better if he left. He turned to leave but found an obstacle in his way.

"Where are you going?" asked the old lady as she blocked Kevin's way.

"Why am I here?" asked Kevin, starting to feel betrayed and trapped.

"Why don't you look and see?" asked the old woman, pointing behind him.

"You mean at the body?" Kevin turned around and looked at the dead person. He really didn't want to have anything to do with whoever was under the covering, but he knew that the old lady wasn't going to let him leave until he looked. He walked over to the body and started to do what he had to. The bandages came off easily and soon the face was shown. It was the one man Kevin didn't want to see. His face was cut up and bleeding but Kevin could still recognize who he was. There was such an anger that rose within him. This person had been dead to him for a long time, and it almost froze his heart to see this person here in front of him now.

"You remember him, don't you, Kevin? His names Chuck, I know you remember, Kevin," said the old lady as she moved behind Chuck. He wasn't dead but looked as if he wished he was. He had been unconscious and couldn't hear much of anything with the bandages on.

"What am I doing here?" asked Chuck in almost a whisper.

"What have you done to him? Why is he here?" asked Kevin, looking at the old woman.

"He has to pay, Kevin. Are you going to let him get away with what he did?" asked the old woman, placing her hand on his face.

"What can I do?"

"Please, let me go," said Chuck, interrupting their conversation.

"Shut up," said the old woman as she hit him on the head and knocked him unconscious again. "Kevin, this man is worth nothing and needs to be deposed of. People like this have to be punished and can't be left alone. What do you think the rest of the world will do? They'll do nothing because they don't care and only want something to be done if it's going to help them. What do you think they would do it if was their brother? People only care about what is theirs and what helps them in life. They no longer care about their friends. It's all about personal gain, and if nothing can be gained then there must be loss. People will do anything not to lose the things they have. They do not know that what they have is pointless and worthless. You must show them the light. They can no longer live this way. We must do something!"

"I don't know," said Kevin, looking at the ground.

"I'll tell you what they would do. They would have killed the man that harmed their brother and no one would have said a thing. They would have just considered it to be right, and who has the power to say what is right and what is wrong? Not anyone here on this earth. I know you don't believe in God and I don't blame you. What has he ever done for you? Killing this man is what you must do, Kevin. There's nothing here to stop you. All you have to do is touch him and command him to die." The old woman moved behind Kevin and lifted his hand in the direction of Chuck.

"You have the touch and no one can stop you. All of it belongs to you." She started to move Kevin closer to the man and soon Kevin was touching him. He wanted Chuck to die more than anything, but he wasn't sure if he should be the one to do it. He had always hoped that one day someone would hit him like he had done his brother and that would be his revenge. He even prayed to God for his death to come and every day he would watch the news to see if he had been killed, but nothing ever turned up.

"Here's your chance to be your own master, Kevin. You have the power to change everything that has given you so much misery. All you have to do is touch him and make him pay. It's just that easy." Kevin just couldn't stop himself. This man's death had driven him crazy and he had just covered it up, but now it had come out and he couldn't stop it. Once Kevin touched Chuck his body started to shake back and forth and soon he fell to the floor. He didn't stop shaking even though he had hit his head hard and Kevin heard the cracking of his skull. After Chuck got back to his feet he grab Kevin to try to stead himself, but Kevin placed his hand on his face and soon all of his skin had melted off of his face. Chuck fell to the ground dead but Kevin still wanted him to suffer more. He placed his hand on him again and his body jumped up off of the ground. Then the body fell back down to the ground and Kevin watched as Chuck's neck released his head and it went rolling over to the other end of the room.

Kevin felt better now that he had done the horrible deed. He didn't think that he had done the right thing, but what did that matter? He had done what he wanted to and gotten justice at the same time. The rest of the world had thought of him as just a little person in a big world, but now he was the big one and the rest of the people would be little in his eyes. Kevin thought of all of this and then realized that he was only doing the thing he hated other people for. He was being a fool and letting his emotion take over him.

"Don't you feel so much better?" the old woman asked Kevin, as she put her hand on his shoulder. Kevin quickly brushed her off.

"This is pointless and I won't be involved. You're on your own," said Kevin as he ran for the exit.

"What do you mean?" said the woman as she grabbed for Kevin to try to stop him. Kevin was angry with himself and with the woman. He couldn't take any more of this and he used his hand to force the woman off of him and into the wall. She almost flew off of the ground and left an indentation in the wall that Kevin had thrown her into.

"You can't do this to me," she said, pulling herself out of the wall, but Kevin had already started crawling out of the room. She knew that she had Kevin and all she had to do was show him what his wife had been up to all of these years. She was sure that would snap him out of this caring about others thing and then he would be all hers. That would put her in control and he wouldn't care about what she made him do. Her plan was coming together better than she had hoped.

Kevin quickly crawled up the stairs and out of the house. He wanted to be happy, but he had never had such a hard time killing anyone. What he had just done felt wrong to him and he couldn't believe that he had done it. He had always told his children that wars were pointless because of the killing that really didn't matter, because in the end everyone would say that it could have all been avoided in the first place. He had never thought about killing someone for no reason. Yes, he had killed his brother, but that still didn't give him the right to kill him. His grandfather had also always told him that two wrongs just leads to ever more trouble and Kevin believe that to be true. He thought his best choice of action was to just get as far away from the house as he could.

He ran down the street and to where he thought that they had parked the car, but he couldn't find it. He didn't know where he was going and he didn't even know where he was. He could have been right next to his neighborhood or he could have been miles away. *I should calm down and look for a bus stop or something,* thought Kevin as he started to walk down the street. Soon Kevin noticed a house that looked familiar. It was the house he had seen in his dreams. He was sure of it and it looked exactly the same. There was the gnome in the yard with the huge and happy smile. There was the blue flower that looked the same as the color of the house and then the side way and the shutters that didn't exactly match. The house looked even better to Kevin in person than it did in the dream. There was a car in the driveway that wasn't there in his dream. Also there was a light on inside and Kevin was sure someone was inside. He didn't know whose house it was, but he had to find out. He slowly made his way up the walkway and to the door. He raised his hand to knock but then he stopped. *What if this is another one of her traps?* thought Kevin as he stopped himself. He looked around for some kind of sign that would have shown him that the old lady was around, but he saw nothing. If she was around Kevin couldn't see her or feel her presence. He would just have to take a chance and see what happened.

Kevin waited for about two minutes after he had knocked before someone came and answer the door. Kevin found someone he thought he would never want to see. It was John. He was wearing his pajamas and had just woken up when Kevin had knocked.

"Hello, Kevin. I knew you would come, but I wasn't expecting you here this early. Come in." John held the door open for Kevin to walk in. Kevin walked past him into the house. He didn't know why but he trusted him for some reason. He felt a lot safer around him than he had for the last few weeks. He still didn't know what he wanted to tell him, but he knew it was time to find out.

"So what brings you here so early?" asked John as he shut the door.

"You told me to come by," said Kevin as he looked around the house. It was mostly empty. Everything was in boxes and looked ready to be shipped out instantly. "Are you moving or something?"

"Yes, I think I've been here long enough. It's time for me to move on and find another place to live."

"Why do you want to leave?"

"I have my reasons." John put his head down as he said this and was quiet for a moment. Kevin didn't want to bother him because he looked as if he was in a lot of pain.

"Are you okay?" asked Kevin after he had waited for a moment.

"Yes, I'm fine," said John, smiling. "Please follow me so we can talk." Kevin followed John through the house and into a room that had a table with two chairs. "I left these here just for you and I to talk," said John as he sat down. "Make yourself at home." Kevin sat down across from him and didn't say much of anything. He wanted to find out about this man and what he had to tell him. He had always thought that it would be some kind of bad news, but now he wasn't so sure.

"How do you like it here, Kevin?" asked John, leaning back in his chair.

"It's okay."

"I never liked this place from the moment I got here. I wish I hadn't come at all and then I wouldn't have to worry about all of this." Kevin didn't know what he was talking about and he figured it was best to not try to rush things and just let the man tell him when he felt like it.

"So why did you come here?" asked Kevin as calmly as he could.

"Well, I had a dream about this place. There was blood everywhere and everything was a mess. I could not believe all of the things that came before me and I quickly woke myself up. I didn't know where all of this was going to happen until I looked at a map. Every time my eyes came across this town I saw the images again, and I was certain that I had to come here and try to stop whatever was going to happen."

"So how did things go?"

"It was all fine at first. I stopped having the dream once I got here and everything seemed peaceful and swell. The church was nice and everybody helped everyone else out when they had a problem. I started to think that the dreams would have only come true if I hadn't have come here and my being here had somehow stopped what was going to happen. That was until my friend died." He paused for a moment and placed his head down on the table. He sounded as if he was crying and Kevin felt sorry for him. He didn't know why but he wanted to try to help this man the best he could. Soon he stopped and looked up at Kevin with blood shot eyes.

"Are you okay?" Kevin asked him as he put his hand on his shoulder to try to comfort him in some way.

"Yes, I'm fine," said John as he wiped his face and continued on with his story. "His name was Carlos Mangle." *This must be the same Carlos Samantha was talking about*, thought Kevin as he listened to John story. "I meet him downtown one night. He owned some people money and he didn't have it on him. He told me that he asked them if he could go and get it, but they wouldn't let him. Then they started to beat him and he was nearly dead by time I found him. The people were still hitting him, but by the grace of the Lord they took off when they saw me coming. I helped Carlos to his feet and brought him to my house. He had a note in his packet that had an address written on it. I thought that maybe I shouldn't have gotten involved, but the Lord told me to go and pay those people before they found out where Carlos was. I prayed for God to show me another way, but there was none." Kevin tried to act as if he cared, but he really didn't. Kevin found this man to be insane. He couldn't see how someone could live in this time frame and believe in such a thing called "God." He could imagine that it might be easier to believe a thousand or so years ago because they weren't as smart as the people nowadays. They lived in clay houses and things of that sort. They didn't know anything about space and time and the other things that are important in this world.

They had an excuse for falling for such tricks and beliefs that talked about God, but nowadays there was no excuse and John just had to be crazy to fall for something like that.

What a fool! What a fool! said a voice to Kevin.

"Soon I found myself downtown paying off some drug dealers for a man that I didn't even know. The only reason I knew his name was because I had looked in his wallet. I almost got shot trying to reason with those dealers. I had never been around such uncivilized people. I could not believe that they felt that they had to live such a life. I didn't see anything that was holding them back from achieving anything that they wanted. They could have lived so much better lives." He placed his head back on the table and began to cry again. *What the hell is wrong with this man?* thought Kevin. He was beginning to grow angry with John. He cried about every little thing and there was certainly nothing he could have done about it. It was their lives and their choices. He should just be happy that he turned out better and move on with life.

He cried for about a minute and Kevin just couldn't take it any longer. "There was nothing that you could have done to help them," said Kevin with as little attitude as he could.

"What do you mean?" asked John, looking up at Kevin.

"They made their choice and they have to live with it. Why should you get involved with anything that they're going to do? Why do you care?"

"Why don't you?" They were quiet for a moment and just looked at each other. Then John talked more about his story.

"I came home to find Carlos awake and trying to steal from me. He dropped everything when he saw me come in and he claimed that it was only for protecting, because he thought that some of his enemy had taken him captive. I told him not to be afraid because I wasn't going to hurt him and only want to help. He was uncomfortable at first but soon he sat down and told me his sad story. He was one of the usually one with abusive parents and being surrounded by the wrong kind of people at the wrong time. He said that he had run away when he was ten and he lived on the streets ever since. I told him that I felt very sorry for him and would do all that I could to try to help." He paused for a moment and it looked as if he was going to cry again, but Kevin shot him a glance and he recovered himself. "After I had made sure that he was okay and didn't have any fatal wounds I told him that I had taken care of his problem and he didn't have to worry about those people any more. He said that he was thankful and asked me if I was an angel sent from God." John laughed as he said this, but stopped once he saw that Kevin didn't find it even the lest amusing. "Well, things came to pass and soon we were best friends and I even got him to go to church. That changed his life and soon he was a man in the eyes of the Lord. He told me that God had given him some kind of gift and he could feel when something was wrong. He told me that something was wrong with the church, but he just didn't know what it was. He told me that he was going to talk to the preacher about it and I didn't hear from him for weeks." John looked as if he was using all of his strength just to keep from crying. Kevin no longer felt sorry for this man that same way he had before. He thought it was sad how he couldn't control his emotions and was so easily crushed. Living a life like his was almost pointless to Kevin. "I went looking for him after I had waited a week and didn't see him at church. I looked at his house and everywhere he had ever told me that he had gone to. I even got the courage to look in the streets, but I found nothing. I prayed and prayed for God to help me find him and soon I did. He had some how turned up in the missing people's section of the paper. I thought that he might have gotten himself back into some kind of trouble and would never hear from him again, but that wasn't so. I got a letter in the mail a couple of days later." He sighed deeply and then slid a piece of paper across the table. "This letter revealed to me everything that he had found and how he had felt. I feel so sorry." John couldn't hold it in any longer and he just had to cry. Kevin looked at him as if he was stupid and quickly opened the letter to reveal its contents. He was amazed at what he found.

Dear John,

I have many things that I need to talk over with you, but it seems as if I don't have much time. I'm sorry that it took me so long to write, but I could not find any other time that seemed right. I came into this world as nobody and with nothing to live for but myself. I thank you for showing me that there was more to life than just drugs and having a good time. I was so blind and I thank you for showing me the light; I don't know what I would have done without you. I would have ended up living a pointless life in a pointless world. I really cannot thank you enough, but I've tried my best. I knew there was something wrong with the church and I was right. I thought that the preacher could have helped me out, but it seems that he was part of the problem. He lives a life worse than mine and doesn't even feel as if he is doing something wrong. I don't understand how he can live talking about what it right and then do exactly what he told others not to do. I don't know if I'm ever going to be able to go back to church again. Well, I don't think I'm going to have to worry about that anyways. I had a vision and in it I confronted Samantha and the preacher. I'd hate to tell you what I saw so just don't expect to hear from me any time soon. I loved being in your company and I thank God that I got the chance to meet you.

Your Friend,

Carlos

P.S. I only wish that there were more time.

"Is he talking about my Samantha?" asked Kevin as he flung the note back across the table. John had placed his head against the table while Kevin was reading and he just shook his head and said yes.

"What did he confront them about?" asked Kevin, beginning to feel angry.

"I…I don't know," said John, looking away from him.

"What do you mean you don't know?"

"I…don't…know." John had barely gotten the words out when Kevin lost he temper. He had put up with all of his talk about nothing and his meaningless story; after all of that this man couldn't even tell him what he wanted to know. There was no way Kevin was going to let him get away with wasting his time for no reason.

Kevin grabbed the bottom of the table and quickly flung it at John. He was in shock and just jumped back against the wall with his mouth open so wide someone could have shoved his or her fist down his throat and wouldn't have even touched his teeth. Kevin wanted to do much worse to him after he gotten what he wanted out of him. He felt as if he would be wrong to allow this man to continue on living in this world believing in such nonsense. Kevin figured that he could just kill him and let him see for himself what was really on the other side. That seemed better than allowing him to torment himself for a God that didn't even exist, right?

Kevin walked across the table he had flipped over and squatted in front of John. He had a smile on his face that terrified the man. It was just the way it looked that sent chills down his spine. That was easy to explain, because the same smile had done that same thing to Kevin only a few days ago. John wasn't entirely afraid though. He feared for his life, but he knew that God wouldn't allow anything to happen to him that he didn't want. Even though John felt as if he should run, he faced his foe with the Lord standing before him.

"I need some answers," said Kevin, "and I think that you're going to give me some."

"Believe me," said John, regaining his courage, "if I had some I would easily give them to you, but I don't. I'm sorry I can't help."

"You have to help me. I need to know."

"Well, then maybe you should go to the church and see what you can find?" They both just looked at each other for a moment and then someone else appeared into the scene.

"You should just kill him," said the old woman sitting in the chair behind Kevin, "you don't need him anymore and he really didn't help you out."

"Why are you here?" Kevin asked the lady as he turned around to face her. John didn't know what was going on. He could feel the presence of the evil woman, but he couldn't see her.

"I had to come and check on you, Kevin. I told you that you couldn't trust that woman."

"Why should I trust you?"

"You don't have to, but—"

She was cut off by John. "Kevin, please don't listen to them. They're evil and only want you go burn in hell with them."

"Tell, me why I should trust you either?" asked Kevin, turning around to look at him.

"You should trust neither of us. You should trust in God to lead you the right way."

"Don't talk about that God nonsense. I should kill you just for believing in that mess."

"Do what you must, but the Lord is on my side."

"Look," said the old woman, getting out of the chair and walking next to Kevin. "He's asking you to kill him. I don't see any reason why you shouldn't. Put this poor fool out of his misery."

"What's in it for you if I kill him?"

"Nothing, but seeing your happiness and pleasure. I only want what you want and nothing else."

"Alright then," said Kevin, smiling, "I guess this is where we say goodbye, John."

"Farewell," said John as he kneeled down and closed his eyes. Kevin raised his hand and pointed it at John. He could feel the power starting to form in his palm and it did make him feel a lot better.

"You see how much better you feel," said the old lady, putting her arms on his shoulders. "This fool doesn't deserve to just die. He must be burned until he's nothing but ashes and then they can just float away in the wind. This fool lived a lie and soon he'll see the truth for himself." As she finished saying this Kevin's arm began to hurt. Then fire appeared around his arm and flew out towards John. It consumed him, but there wasn't any kind of pain or screaming coming out of him. At first Kevin just took the pain and kept the fire under control, but soon it became too much to bear. The flames started to go everywhere. By now John was nothing but ashes.

"You need to get out of here fast, Kevin," said the old lady. "I'll meet you outside." Then she disappeared. *She couldn't even wait for me to get out,* thought Kevin. Kevin worked his way through the house, but he couldn't find the door. It continued to become hotter and hotter and Kevin knew the house wouldn't last much longer. Soon he just gave up looking for the door and just ran through the wall. He had to hit it three times before he could break through, but once he made it through he ran as fast as he could from the house and the fire. He made it around the corner only a few moments before the firemen showed up. He stopped and looked at the house at the very same moment that it collapsed. If he had had X-ray vision he would have seen something beyond belief happening inside of the house.

"Did anyone see you?" said the old lady, standing behind Kevin.

"I don't think so," after he said this he leaned forward to catch his breath.

"Come on," said the old lady, grabbing Kevin, "we have to get out of here. Soon the police will be here and then there'll be a mess. You don't live over here so you'll be the number one suspect if anyone see you." She started to pull him, but he barely moved. Every part of his body was in pain. He felt as if something was inside of him and was trying to tear him apart. He had been through lots of pain during his life but none of it could compare to what he felt now. He didn't know it was possible for anyone to feel so much pain all at one time.

"Hurry, Kevin," said the old lady as she continued to try to pull him. "I can also feel the pain that you are feeling, but that's only natural. It means that…it means that you passing over; that you have finally learned how to use the touch. Once you get through this there will be nothing to stop you from getting your revenge on you wife and anyone else you want to harm. I'm here for you, Kevin, and you're going to have to trust me if you want to get out of here." She stopped pulling on him and looked him in the face. "You can do this, Kevin, I know you can."

Kevin didn't trust her, but he felt as if he had to give into her if he ever wanted to get rid of this pain.

"Where did all of this pain come from?"

"I already told you."

"Yes, then why can you get rid of it?"

"Well…you have to get rid of it yourself. If I did it for you…you wouldn't know that you were able to control it. Kevin, you have to pull yourself together so we can get out of here." Kevin closed his eyes and used all of his strength to put the pain at bay so he could move. "There I told you that you could do it."

"I can't move for long so let's move quickly." Soon they made there way through the town and into the dead end that the old lady had hidden the car in earlier. The car was there and looked just like it had before. Kevin thought that the old lady must have made it look like the dead end had disappeared because she wanted him to stay and kill John before he left. He began to wonder if it was him or her who was in control.

They quickly got into the car and then the old lady backed out of the dead end. They didn't talk as they drove down the street that lead to the end of the town, and Kevin looked back just in time to see an explosion of in the distance. He couldn't believe his eyes. He knew that the explosion may have harmed many people, but he really didn't care about that. What he wanted to know was if it was his hand that had done it or if it was something else.

Once they were out of the town Kevin turned to ask the old lady, but she already knew what he was going to say.

"You want to know if that was you who did all of that, don't you?" said the old lady, putting on her smile again.

"Yes," said Kevin, holding his right arm.

"Well, I guess I should tell you the truth. The only reason you're in so much pain is because you used too much energy at one time. I wouldn't be surprised if you died right here in this car." She paused and looked at Kevin. As she did this he screamed because the pain that he had blocked came back almost instantly. It felt even worse than it had before and the old lady put her hand on him and tried to suppress his pain, but there wasn't much she could do; in fact, there was nothing that she could do. She didn't even know where the pain was coming from and whenever she tried to read his thoughts the pain would just spread to her and she couldn't even take half of the pain that he was going through. She thought at first that his body was going to reject her, but she figure that she was already too deep inside of him for that to happen. All he had to do was open the door and she would have control over everything.

"Kevin, hold on," said the old lady, "I'm going to take you somewhere and do something about your pain." Kevin didn't hear much of what she was saying because he fainted a few moments later.

"Kevin...Kevin, what's wrong?" The old lady shook him but he still didn't respond. She knew she had to take him to some place where she could try to help him in some kind of way even though she wasn't sure of what she could do. The closest and safest place for her to take him was his parents' house. She knew that he might not feel happy going there, but if he died it wouldn't matter.

It took her about five minutes to get there and she quickly got him out of the car. The house was almost completely ruined. The old lady would have kicked the door in, but it wasn't there anymore. Inside there was a couch but it looked as if something had been chewing into it but then decided to leave the rest for someone or something else. She decided not to lay him there and continued on through the house. Soon she came into the kitchen and found a table. She quickly cleaned it off and then she placed Kevin on it.

She went on examining his body and even tried to look into his mind but something blocked her from doing anything. She couldn't allow him to die. There weren't many people who could use the touch like Kevin just had; in fact, Kevin was the only person that the old lady had even been allowed to go so deep inside of. He was like a desert and the old lady had found water and made herself wealth. She wasn't sure of what made him so valuable, but she couldn't risk anything happening to him. She put her head on his chest and began to cry. She wasn't sad or anything, but she just hoped that somehow that would help him. Though she cried her heart out, nothing happened. She didn't know why she had thought that would work and she would have laughed at herself if someone else hadn't done it for her.

"You aren't the one to act like a fool," said someone, laughing behind the old lady.

"Why are you here, Brian?" said the old lady as she turned around and looked at him. It was the little child with the gray skin. He wasn't wearing anything, but a pair of pants and he looked as skinny as a stick. His teeth were as black as space and looked as if they would fall out at any minute. If Kevin had been awake he would have preferred to look at the hideous old woman than to look at him.

"I thought you might need some help on this one. He is different from the rest."

"Yes, I know this. That is why I have to keep him alive. I can not let him die," said the old lady, trying to think of something she could do.

"Do you even know what is wrong?" asked Brian, smiling.

"I haven't a clue."

"I hope this isn't part of you plan or do you really know nothing about what is happening. Either way it's funny to watch you act like such a fool. Why I would never..." Before he could finish the old lady cut him off. She had no tolerance for such nonsense and she despised being ridiculed and made a fool of. She had raised her hand while he was talking and sent him flying into the wall almost making him go through it. Brain didn't feel any of the pain but his strength was nothing compared to the old lady's. Soon he got back to his feet and smiled.

"I didn't mean to offend you. I was only pointing out the obvious. You don't have a clue about what is going to happen to him and he may even die. What will you do then?"

"That just can't happen. I won't let it."

"You know I think that maybe HE had something to do with this."

"What do you mean?"

"I saw everything that happened and maybe you shouldn't have killed that man. He may have been important."

"There aren't many people still alive who have any importance in HIS eyes. There's no reason for him to care about Kevin. Kevin has done nothing for HIM to even notice him; otherwise, I would have just allowed Rachel to hold on to the touch instead of giving it to him. HE is not going to mess this up for me. I won't let HIM."

"Is there anything you can do if HE wants to interfere?"

"No there's nothing I can do, but Kevin can do something about HIM. I only need to take him a little farther and then nothing will be able to stop me."

"What if he changes his mind and doesn't want to help you?" said Brian, smiling again.

"That won't happen."

"Yes, and I bet you thought that this wouldn't happen either."

"Get out of here! I don't feel like being tormented by your presence."

"Well, I'll leave, but what are you going to do about Kevin?"

"It's none of your concern."

"You would think that, wouldn't you, but what if I have a cure."

"What do you mean?" asked the old woman as she walked towards him.

"I might know a spell that should free him, but it going to cost you."

"Are you telling the truth?" said the old woman, starting to take him seriously and walking towards him.

"Who knows? What do you have to lose?"

"If it works you can have anything that you want. I mean as long as I can give it to you."

"Well then let's get to work," said Brian, putting on the biggest smile he was capable of making.

Kevin woke up with a headache. He opened his eyes to find himself in an unfamiliar place. The table that he was lying on looked as if it would collapse any minute and Kevin quickly jumped off of it. There wasn't much in the house and Kevin looked for a way out. Soon he came to a room that had a couch in it. It looked nasty and Kevin couldn't imagine anyone trying to sit on it. He started to leave the room when he saw his mother sitting on the couch.

She looked even more beautiful than Kevin had remembered her. She sat there on the couch as if nothing had even happened and soon it appeared that way. Everything that was nasty and worn out returned to normal and the house looked like a paradise. The color returned to the walls and the house was full of all the things Kevin remembered that used to be within the house. Soon she got up to answer the door. Three little kids came running through the door with presents. She took the presents from then and pointed to the other room of the house. They quickly left her and ran into the other room. She then walked over to a table and laid the presents down. A little child can running out of the room that the other kids had just entered. He ran up to her and pulled on her skirt and looked as if he was trying to tell her something. She shook her head and pointed back towards the room. He quickly left and she put her hand on her head as if she was in some kind of pain. Kevin wanted to walk over and comfort her, but before he could she walked over to the couch and pulled out a bottle from inside of the cushion. It was wine and she quickly put it to her mouth. She drunk the whole bottle in a couple of seconds and Kevin could tell that she was drunk. As if on cue a policeman walked in through the door and towards her. He said something and she grabbed him and pulled him down to her. She put her lips against his and kissed him for about half a minute. After she was done kissing him she started to undress him and he started to do the same to her. The child that had pulled on her skirt earlier came back into the room and tried to speak with her, but the man hit him. She looked at the child and was going to say something, but the man kissed her again and she forgot about it.

Kevin had grown angry watching the scene. He couldn't stand her being drunk and then that man being on top of her. He couldn't just stand there and allow that man to hit that child for no reason. Kevin felt as if he could kill that man and maybe even her. *Why had she just stood there and let that man do that?* thought Kevin. Was that not her child and her blood? She was supposed to protect him and keep him secure, but instead she didn't do anything. Kevin's angry grew until he could no longer control it. He didn't have time to think about what he was going to do and the next thing he knew he had flipped the couch. The people who where sitting on the couch didn't seem to notice that Kevin had flipped the couch; in fact, they just up and disappeared along with everything else. The house changed back from a paradise in to a wasteland. Kevin's anger left just as quickly as it had come and now he felt different. He was sad. He wished that he could some how reverse the memories that he had and started over, but he knew that wasn't possible. He fell to his knees in the same spot that the couch had been and cried. He couldn't help himself and he just had to let it out. He remembered times when he had scolded himself for crying and other times he had laughed at his friends. He never thought he would be so feeble and have such a hard time controlling his emotions. He just couldn't hold any of it in anymore and he pounded his hand on the ground as hard as he could. Soon the ground couldn't hold Kevin's weight and the front of his body went through the ground and Kevin barely caught himself before he fell in.

He had to struggle to pull himself up, but he made it. Kevin looked at the hole and he saw that it had already been made. Someone had fallen through and then patched it back up again. Kevin didn't know why anyone would even be inside of this grisly place, but he decided to look into the hole anyways. He could not see much of anything because it was shadowy, but there was an atrocious scent coming out of it. Kevin promptly jumped back and enclosed his nose. He knew that there was only one thing that could give off a smell that unpleasant and that was putrid human flesh. Kevin knew that someone must have killed someone else or more than one person and hid his or her bodies in the floor of the house. Kevin really thought that he should just leave it alone and he was going to but something told him that too many people had already died inside of this house and it didn't need anymore. He covered his nose with his shirt and went into the hole, looking for the body.

He couldn't see anything and there were many other things under the hole that just a body or bodies. Kevin could feel rats crawling over his hands every now and then. There were also many bugs and other things that Kevin was sure weren't a body but he still couldn't classify them. Soon he ran into something that he had almost hoped not to find, but knew that he would. He was relieved that it was inside of a trash bag and he didn't have to physically touch it. The smell grew even worse as he began to pull it, but he knew that it would be over soon and then he could get away from it. The bag was heavy and every now and then it would get caught on something and he'd have to pull twice as hard to get it loose. It got caught on something right before Kevin began to lift it out. Kevin pulled with all of his strength and he would have gotten the bag and all of its contents out if it hadn't ripped.

The contents of the bag fell through the tear and back into the hole. Kevin had still been pulling and he fell back as the bag became very light. Kevin had been pulling so hard that he couldn't stop himself as he fell back and he would have ran into the wall if someone hadn't stopped him. Kevin raised his eyes to look at his savior and found the old woman smiling. She then let him go and he hit the ground hard. The old lady studied him and then she caught sight of the bag that he had clenched in his hands.

"Are you okay, my dear?" asked the old lady as she leaned forward towards Kevin's face.

"I'm fine," said Kevin as he grunted and got to his feet.

"I'll glad to see that you're okay. I thought that something terrible might have happened to you."

"Well, whatever you did I must thank you."

"There's no need for that. What were you up to?"

"I was…getting something out of that hole."

"Can you tell me what you were getting?"

"Yes…I smelled something and I knew that it had to been a body decaying or something so I decided to look and see if it was true."

"Well was it?"

"I don't know. We should go and find out." They both began to walk over to the hole. Kevin had to cover his mouth as they got closer, but the old lady continued to breathe and smile as if she found the smell pleasant and not spiteful. Kevin thought that maybe she had killed this person so Kevin could find it and she could some how torment him. Then he thought that she really hadn't tormented him at all. He knew that deep down inside all of the things he had already done he had wanted them to happen. Of course that didn't make it right, but what could he do about it now. The old woman just wanted to help him get rid all of that stress instead of holding in his emotions and to help him become a better person. How could he blame her for that?

Soon they had made it to the hole. Kevin looked down, but he still couldn't see much of anything. The old woman, on the other hand, could see everything perfectly and was delighted by what she saw.

"Well I guess you were right," said the old woman as she smiled into the hole.

"What do you mean?"

"Don't you see it?" asked the old lady as she pointed into the hole.

"No, I'm sorry. I can't see much of anything inside of this hole. What exactly do you see?"

"Well it's kind of hard to explain. Why don't I just show it to you." Before Kevin could even answer her, she quickly put her hand into the hole. Then she dug around for a moment as if she was looking for something of importance and not touching what Kevin believe to be a dead body. Soon her smile widened and she pulled her hand from out of the hole.

"Here we are," she said as a head emerged from the hole. Kevin quickly turned his face away because he couldn't stand to see it. There were bugs crawling inside and outside of it. The hair was falling out and looked almost entirely gone. The skin looked molded and green like apiece of old bread that's been thrown on the floor and never picked up. Even though all of this was horrible that's not what was frightening Kevin and made him looked away. What scared him was that the head belong to someone he knew. It was Samantha's head.

"Please put it away," said Kevin as he fell to his knees and tried to keep himself from throwing up. His stomach felt as if it would burst if he didn't and he felt as if he could pass out at any minute. His mind was running through millions of questions and Kevin couldn't find any answers. Why was she here? Who could have done it? Why would they have done it? Was that the reason that he could stand to be around her? Where were her faith and her God now?

"Are you sure that you don't want to see it?" said the old woman, still smiling and carrying on.

"How can you be so cruel?"

"What do you mean?"

"I mean how can you treat people this way. I understand that you might have had as bad of a life as I have, but she didn't do anything to you and she didn't deserve to die this way. There was no need and it was just pointless. You should feel ashamed."

"You think that I did this? Why is that?"

"I don't know anyone else that would have wanted to kill her."

"How do you know it's a her? I can't tell if it's anyone that I want to kill so how do you know?"

"Why must you constantly speak so many lies? You and I both know who that is?"

"Well could you tell me because I can not recognize who this skull could belong to?"

"It belongs to…" But Kevin stopped. *Skull. What was she talking about?* thought Kevin. He had not seen any of her skull and didn't think that the old lady would have pealed her skin off. Were they both talking about the same thing? Kevin needed to know but was once again terrified as he turned around to look. He didn't find anything close to what he had thought he would find. There weren't any bugs and there wasn't any hair. The skin was gone and all that was left was a skull that could have belonged to anyone that had been relieved of his or her skin. Kevin was shocked, but happy at the same time. Samantha was still alive and he didn't have to worry or know whom that skull belonged to.

"So what were you saying?" asked the old woman, looking at Kevin as if he was crazy, which she thought he was.

"Nothing," said Kevin, putting his head down, "I must have been imagining that something was there that wasn't. I'm sorry for talking to you like I did."

"Well you should be. I didn't even do anything."

"I really am. Will you forgive me?"

"Yes, of course," said the old woman while she put the skull down and smiled. She knew what Kevin had seen and what he had felt. The only problem was that Kevin didn't even have a clue.

"So how do you think it got here?" asked Kevin.

"I really don't know or care. Maybe it is a homeless person or someone that did drugs and owned someone money. You know things like this happen all of the time and they have nothing…" Kevin was thinking to hard to pay any attention to the rest of what she had to say. He had thought of Carlos when she mentioned the drugs and wondered if it could be him. There was no way of knowing for sure unless he could find a reason why he had been brought here.

"Why do you think that they would have put him or her in a bag instead of just throwing them in here? In fact, they didn't even have to cover up the hole."

"Who knows? Maybe they had to transport the person here and then they hid whoever it is. They might have been trying to make sure that no one looked for the body. Some people are just cautious like that." Kevin had been thinking while she said that also and he remembered seeing a bag somewhere, but now he just couldn't think of where he had seen it. He thought for a moment and entirely blocked out the old lady. She had been talking and noticed that he wasn't listening. She knew he was in deep thought and decided to read his mind. She had known exactly where to find the information that he was looking for and she quickly put it to the front of his mind.

"Yes," said Kevin, "I remember a dream in which I saw someone bringing a bag to this house, but who could it have been?"

"I remember you having that dream. Wasn't it Samantha who was driving the car and opened the trunk?" Kevin eyes opened as wide as they possible could. He remembered it perfectly and there was no doubt in his mind about who had brought the body to the house.

"But why do you think she would do this?" asked Kevin, looking at the old woman.

"I don't know. Maybe she killed him and brought him here to hide the body."

"But who would she have to kill?" Almost immediately after he had finished his question he knew the answer. There was only one person that stood out in his mind that Samantha would have reason to kill. Carlos. He knew something about her and she wanted to keep it a secret. Kevin had thought that maybe he was wrong about his deduction, but then the old lady showed him the memory of his missing shotgun. *Samantha must have used that*, thought Kevin, *but I never thought that she would be capable of doing such a thing.*

156

"I need to get out of here," said Kevin as he got to his feet.

"But where are you going?" asked the old lady, getting up to follow him.

"I need to look into something. I want you to let me do this alone."

"Well, okay. I only want you to be pleased."

"That would please me very much," said Kevin as he left the house. For the first time he thought that he was doing something on his own and by his own will. He felt free and as if he had control of the old lady and of the touch. He didn't know what he would find, but he was prepared for the worst. The old lady thought it would be useless to follow him because she had planned for him to go alone and knew of what he would find. All she had to do was show up when the killing started.

Kevin jumped inside of the car and drove towards his destination. He knew it would take him about thirty minutes to get there and by then it would be around one o'clock. He was almost positive that it was Sunday and he knew that Samantha would be where he was going. He didn't know what he was going to do, but he figured that would all come to him when he got there. He was lucky that there weren't any policemen out because he was driving over eighty miles an hour and didn't even stop at any of the stop signs or lights. Even if he had been paying attention to them he wouldn't have stopped. His mind was too occupied with the idea of what he might find. He knew that he would regret ever wanting to come in the first place, but he couldn't imagine going on in this world living with his wife while she lied to him. If she really had killed Carlos that was something Kevin would learn to live with if there was a good enough reason. He wouldn't tell a soul and they could just continue living without every having to speak about it again.

Soon he came to the place which he loathed entirely. He had never thought that he would have to come back to his place and he never thought he would want to. He still wasn't sure if he could walk in and he just sat in his car for about three minutes. Then he made up his mind that nothing bad was going to happen, because there was nothing anyone or anything could do to him. It was all phony anyways, right?

The building seemed to stare at Kevin as he got out of the car. It was as if something didn't want him to enter the place and would never allow it.

There were many people walking out of the church, but none of them took any notice to Kevin. He felt invisible among such people and thought it was best that he wasn't noticed. The people seemed happy and Kevin didn't want to speak with any of them about anything good. For all he knew many of them already knew about what he was trying to find and had kept it a secret from him. If he ever found this to be true he would make sure that they were killed and never thought of again.

Soon the people lessened and almost all of the cars were gone. The door to the building had been left open and Kevin walked in making sure he didn't touch it. As he looked around he felt himself wanting to close his eyes. This placed was considered to be very holy, but Kevin could see nothing holy about it. He considered it to be a waste of time and money. It was pointless and he just couldn't understand why someone would ever want to believe in such a thing as God. He thought it was wrong for people to disgrace themselves in the manner that they did for some anonymous deity. They talked about such things as the Holy Spirit and speaking in tongues. They'd put on a good act and jump around, waving their arms, and murmuring as if they were speaking some kind of language. Kevin remembered a time when he had acutely believed that it all was true; that there was a God and a Holy Spirit; when he thought it was possible to move mountains and do anything with the grace of the Lord behind you. He had prayed every night and every morning for his father to come home and for things to get better. It wasn't all in vain though, his father did come home and in a sense things did get better. His mother may have died and his father didn't even speak to him, but he took a serial killer off of the streets and maybe saved many other people. That mattered to Kevin but he could not take much of it. That wasn't what he had prayed would happen and he stopped believing in God for a while. He went around doing thing that he would have never done before; killing, stealing, cursing, having sex, and defiling himself in every way he knew how. He even put a table with the Ten Commandments over his bed and every time he broke one he would put a mark next to it. There was one that he couldn't break or obey if he wanted to. He just put a mark through it and never looked at it again.

He continued to live his life like this for a while not caring what other people thought of him. All he wanted was to be left alone and to do his own thing. There was nothing anyone could offer him to relieve the pain that he was going through; well, no one but God. It was the very same priest that worked at the church that Kevin was standing in that came up to him and set him straight. Of course it didn't happen all at once but soon Kevin was going back to church and he even started singing in the choir. His faith in God began to grow and he started to believe in what he now found impossible. He started to give and bless everyone that he came in contact with. He read his Bible and carried it with him always. There was nothing that was going to keep him from church or from his new life. It all seemed great, until he found out the truth about his mother and the doctor.

Kevin noticed two people at the altar on their knees doing what appeared to be praying. He started to remember times when he had done that same thing, but he stopped himself. He wished he could forget everything he had ever done in church. It constantly haunted him and he felt as if he would have it with him the rest of the life. If he still believed he would have prayed to God to release him from his torment.

Kevin knew that it was rude to interrupt someone while they was in deep thought, but he really didn't care now.

"Hello," said Kevin as he walked closer to the two by the altar. They didn't answer him and acted as if they couldn't hear him. Kevin then remembered that when he used to pray it was hard to hear the things around you. Kevin thought that they were just in deep thought and he would have to shake them or something to wake them up. This would have been true if they really had been praying. Kevin walked a little closer and said hello again, but it was the same as before. Kevin felt as if he would dirty himself by touching anyone while they were inside of this place, but he didn't have many other options.

"Hello, uh can you help me with something?" Kevin asked as he shook one of them. They looked up at him and Kevin saw his eyes. They were blank and as white as snow. Kevin had never seen anything like this. Yes, he had seen some strange things these past few days, but that was all nothing compared to what he was seeing now. There was so much power inside of his eyes that it frightened Kevin. He had never in his life been this afraid of anything. He was always a man that would stand up and face his fears, but now he felt helpless. He wanted to run and hide somewhere, but something internal told him that he should stay.

Soon the man's eyes returned to normal and he stood up and looked at Kevin who just stood with his mouth open.

"Hello," said the man, "do you need something?"

Kevin quickly closed his mouth and said, "I…I wanted to know if you could help me with something."

"Well, if I can I will. This is God's house and it's open to everyone."

What a fool, thought Kevin.

"I want to know where I can find the preacher. I just moved here and I'm eager to become saved. That is what you people do, right?"

"Yes, my brother. You have come to the right place and you will find what you are looking for. If the preacher finds that you are able, you know what to do, don't you?" Kevin didn't have a clue about what he was talking about. He was going to just say no, but the man winked at him and Kevin thought that it was best to just say yes and move on.

"I see that we understand each other," said the man, winking again, "if you go to the right you will find a long hallway. Turn to the left and go down five doors. It will be the only black door in the hallway. You'll have to knock about three times and then you need to say the password. You were already informed about that information, right?"

"Yes," said Kevin very slowly not knowing what he was talking about. The man looked at Kevin with a face that said, "Why don't you tell me what it is." Kevin thought quickly of all kind of things that he could possibly say that he hoped might be the code, but it was pointless. The man soon said that he was going to ask him for the code, but that it wasn't necessary at the time because he couldn't remember the code himself. If Kevin was a man of God he would have thanked Him with all of his soul, but instead he just smiled and walked away.

He walked down the hallway just as the man had told him. Soon he came to the black door and he stopped. He didn't know the code so he couldn't just walk in. He decided to try to find another way. He walked over to the next door and found that it was unlocked. He walked in and looked around. It was empty except for brown bags. There were lots of them and they went almost to the ceiling. Kevin walked over to them and he tried to open one. It took him awhile, but he finally got it. He hadn't expected everything that was inside to come falling out on to his feet. He tried to move but it didn't work. His shoes were covered with the stuff and he tried to wipe it off, but it only went into the air and into his breath. He instantly knew what it was and was almost shocked, but then he reminded himself that he had known it was a fake house and this only gave him another reason to believe it to be so.

He was amazed to find that a large amount of the stuff had gone up his noise, but he wasn't affected like he should have been. Times before when he had taken it he only needed half of what had just gone up his noise to get high and now he couldn't feel anything. There wasn't even a slight buzz of sensation. Kevin thought that maybe it was fake and they just wanted people to think that it was real, but after he tried it again he was sure of what it was.

Kevin walked away from the bags and over to the right side of the room. He was hoping to find some kind of door that connected the two rooms and he did. He was glad that it was unlocked and he walked through trying to hide himself from anyone that might have been in the other room. He didn't find anyone. In fact he wasn't even in a room. He could not see where he was, but he reached out anyways. His hand came in contact with some material, but he wasn't sure of what it was. He then reached out his other hand and continued to feel the material. Then it came to him. It was a shirt. He moved his hands along and they came across more of them. *I must be in a closet*, thought Kevin.

He walked through the clothes and found himself at the door of the closet. He was going to open it, but he heard voices coming from the other side. He knew one of them, but the others were new to him.

"So how is everyone today?" asked Samantha. "Phillip, did you miss me?"

"Of course, I'm always thinking of you," answered Phillip.

"Well, I don't mean to be in the way," said the other person that was in the room, "but I have something I need to talk over with you, Preacher."

"Well, okay."

"It's private and I would not want the information to fall into the wrong hands."

"What do you mean? Samantha is the trustworthiest person in this church. If there's anything that you can tell me then you'll be able to tell her also. I trust her more than I trust you." Kevin could hear something that sounded like a kiss. He could not tell if it was on the cheek or the lips, but it didn't matter much to him. Either way there was something going on between them and Kevin had to find out what.

"Well, if you're sure, Preacher," said the other man.

"Yes, I'm sure and if you don't stop wasting my time I might have to get rid of you."

"Okay, I thought that you would need to know that the shipment of cocaine has come in, but we don't have much more room."

"What do you mean? All of the room inside of the rooms and the altar are filled."

"Yes, we need some new places."

"Well, I'm sure that you'll find something."

"We tried, but have failed to come up with anything."

"Well—"

"I'll think of something for you," said Samantha, cutting Phillip off.

"Thank you," said the other man, "I don't wish to waste any more of your time."

"Well, then leave!" said Phillip and then Kevin heard the door close. Now was the time of truth in which Kevin would find out what was going on other than the drugs. He almost decided to get up and leave so he wouldn't have to face the true, but he told himself that he had to know. If it were what he feared then he would just have to live with it. He could find a way to forgive Samantha, but he would make sure that Phillip died before he had the chance to see her again. He usually would have had some kind of bad feeling about doing something bad to a preacher, but from what he could tell he wasn't a real one. He was just a fool that would soon be struck down by Kevin's wrath. He told himself that if it wasn't what it seemed he might just let that man live, but then he decided that sooner or later it would lead to what he didn't want and it would be better to just kill him now. So it was time for Kevin to just sit and listen.

"Now that we're here all alone what are you here for?" asked Phillip.

"I need to talk to you about something very important."

"Well, you know you can talk to me about anything. I'm here for you just as God is. You know I love you." That last sentence was too much for Kevin. He froze when he heard him say that even though that wasn't the important part. Kevin wanted to know if Samantha would say it back to him. If that was to happen he didn't know what he would do. He could already feel his arm being to grow in power, but he constrained himself until he could hear her answer.

"Yes, I know," said Samantha.

Everything was quiet for a moment and then Phillip said, "Do you love me too?" This was what Kevin had been waiting for. The words that came out of Samantha's mouth after this would decide between what Kevin was going to do. Something inside of Kevin almost wanted to cover his ears so he would never know what had happened, but he had to know.

"You know that I—" said Samantha.

"I know that you what!" said Phillip. Kevin heard a sound and he thought that maybe Phillip had hit Samantha against something and knocked her unconscious, but then he heard her speak.

"You know that I can't do this with you. What if Kevin finds out? What are you going to do then?"

"What about Kevin? I don't see him here holding you in his arms and crying at your feet. I don't think he could ever love you as much as I do. There is nothing I would not do for you. Why, I'll even kill Kevin if I have to."

"What do you mean kill?"

"I'll cut his throat, I'll rip out his heart, I'll do anything that will please you and make you stay with me. All you have to do is say the word."

"I can not allow you to do something like that. Though you may love me more than Kevin does now, there was a time when we were greatly in love. I couldn't let you kill him."

"What about a divorce then? You could come and live with me and leave him behind you. He it's good for anything anyways. He doesn't love you anymore and it's a waste of your time to stay with him."

"I don't know. I've already mess up once—"

"Be quiet. You never need to speak about that again. That is in your past and I know that you'll never do that again. The Lord and I have forgiven you. You are redeemed from any sin that you have ever committed and will ever commit. I myself have said so. It must be done and followed. You have nothing to worry about."

"Thank you for forgiving me and helping me to reach God. I see that you are right and I will think about what you have said." Kevin heard footsteps going towards the door. Soon others followed.

"Are you going to leave now?" asked the preacher.

"I have to. What about my children?"

"They will be fine. Let God watch over them. I want you to be here with me."

"You mean that you want to—"

"Yes you know what I want and I'm not taking no for an answer. You know that everything good in life comes with a price. Even God." Everything was quiet for a moment and then Kevin could hear zippers unzipping. He stood there shocked. He just couldn't believe that something like that was going to happen. The only way he could make himself believe it was for him to look and see. The bottom of the door was in a good enough angle for Kevin to watch most of what was going on, but until now he didn't feel as if he needed to use it. He slowly leaned forward until the light of the room hit his eyes. He had to scan the room, but soon he found what he was looking for. It abhorred him and his body went numb almost instantly. He couldn't believe what he was seeing though he had almost expected to find it. He wanted to burst through the door and kill both of them, because seeing Samantha do this just sent him over the edge. He didn't know if he could ever bring himself to forgive her of something like this.

Kevin watched for a moment and then he made up his mind to kill them and just get it over with, but when he tried to move he couldn't. He couldn't turn his head or close his eyes. He was completely paralyzed and he couldn't do much of anything. Kevin wanted to scream, but he couldn't do that either. He could not understand what was happening to him. This was the worst time for him to be stuck in one place looking at something that he didn't want to see, but there was almost nothing he could do about it. He tried to just think of something else, but that didn't help anything. He sat there for almost an hour looking at the two of them with his anger growing the entire time. It started to overcome him and soon it took control. He didn't care what happened to Samantha or Phillip or even the church. He was going to kill everything that got in his ways and would show no mercy.

"I think that it's time for me to go," said Samantha, putting back on her clothes.

"Are you going to come back tomorrow?" asked Phillip, putting his on also.

"I don't know. I'm not sure of what the children are doing or about Kevin, though after that experience we just had I don't think getting rid of him will be a problem."

"Are you serious? You're not playing with me."

"No, I think it would be better getting him out of my life. I could even leave him the kids."

"You would do all of that," said Phillip with much passion.

"Yes."

"Yes? Yes, and then we could start our own life and buy a new house. It will just be you and me forever."

"Forever." Then they kissed each other for about a minute or two. After that Samantha grabbed her things and left the room. Kevin would have come out of the closet, but he was still in shock. He couldn't believe that she had said something like that. Kevin had given up everything for her and she didn't even care. She was just going to leave him and the children for some fake preacher that wasn't worth a thing. He was a bum that would first pleasure his lustrous heart and then he would leave her out in the cold. When that happened she would be on her own, because Kevin would never want to see her again.

Kevin sat there thinking about the things that had just occurred before him. He had been in this same position for about two hours and he couldn't feel any kind of pain or agony. Phillip never noticed him and he was happy that soon he would get what he wanted. He cared for Samantha, but what he wanted more was Kevin's death. Samantha had told Phillip, right before she left, that Kevin had almost two million dollars of insurance and his death would help them out a lot. Phillip said that he could pay back many of his debts and get back on his feet. Kevin knew that then he would ditch Samantha and never see her again.

"That woman is such an idiot," said Phillip as he looked through his desk for something. "It's never been this easy for me to trick someone and take everything that they had. At least this one is fine and not fat and ugly. Lord, I do have to thank you for all of this also." Phillip then looked up into the sky and laughed. He had his eyes closed and the sound of his laugh was so loud that he couldn't see or hear Kevin walking up behind him. Though Kevin wanted to massacre him he felt as if he should play around with him first and make him suffer.

"Hello, Preacher," said Kevin, putting his mouth close enough to his ear that he could have kissed him. Before the man could answer him Kevin grabbed the bottom of his chair and pulled back. Phillip was flung forward into his desk. His face hit and then he fell over to the ground. He hadn't suffered much damage but there was a long slash across his face.

"Who...who are you?" asked Phillip, trying to crawl away from him. He was almost too scared to move and was trembling so much that he almost couldn't move at all. Kevin just smiled and laughed at him. He couldn't believe that Samantha was in love with such a feeble man. He couldn't even stand up on his two feet and die like a man. Kevin had gone to war and back, but this man had spent his life cheating and killing people. What a fool!

"So how have things been?" asked Kevin, walking closer to his opponent.

"I don't know you. How do you know me? I've never seen you at church," said the preacher, looking around for a way out.

"And you never will. I would never come to your church. I can't see why you would want to go. It's pointless and everyone who believes in such things should be killed. You are pathetic!" Kevin grabbed a bottle off of the table and threw it at him. He didn't even see it coming and it hit him on the side of his face. He had not looked that good to begin with and this did not help any. Kevin then stared at his face trying to decide which side looked worse. He never came to a conclusion.

"I don't understand why you are doing this and I don't want to. I only ask that we sit down and talk about this."

"There isn't much to talk about. You and I both know why I'm here and I think you can guess what I'm going to do to you."

"Look," said Phillip as he tried to get to his feet, but Kevin pushed him back down, "there is no need for all of this violence. I have lots of money and I know that I can find enough of it to please you and then we can put this all behind us."

"So you're saying that you're going to pay me to leave you alone and forget about this?"

"Yes, and what ever else you want. I will spare no expense to see that you leave here happily."

"And why would I stop there? Why wouldn't I come back and take more and more of your money? If money was the problem then this could be fixed without me taking your life, but that is not the case."

"What do you mean? Money can solve anything. Money keeps the world going and can make a person do anything that you want them to. Why wouldn't it work now?"

"Because I have no need for money, and all I want is your life. I'm not going to leave this place until I make sure that you are dead. Then I will be satisfied."

"But what is this about? As the Lord has me witness—"

"Why don't you shut up? I can not stand to hear your voice. You are going to pay for what you did and there is nothing that will stop me. Tell the Lord that and see what happens." Kevin then took another step towards Phillip. He didn't even move this time. He was too scared. His body was aching and his heart skipped every other beat. He had never felt such pain. His body felt as if it would fall apart at any moment and there was nothing he could do about it. Kevin could feel his power growing and knew that he was in control.

"I don't understand why you believe in such a thing as God anyways. It's pointless. If there was such a thing as God then why would he allow things like this to happen? The only thing God is good for is to make money as you have already pointed out." Kevin put his face just a few inches in front of Phillip's. "So what do you have to say?"

Phillip's heart just stopped and he didn't know what to say. Words just came out of his mouth.

"I don't understand—"

Kevin cut him off. "Of course you don't understand. You're primitive, you're useless, you're futile, you're a waste of time, you're mindless, you're lost, you're unnecessary, and you're human. But it's not your fault," said Kevin, lifting Phillip off of the ground with one hand. Kevin had never felt this much power in his entire life. He felt as if he could destroy the world. He felt as if nothing else matter but what he was doing. He had made up his mind that this foolish man in front of him was never going to see another day on this earth.

"You can't help but be a fool. You grew up like this and there's nothing you can do about it. Some things just can't be helped and this is one of them." Kevin swung Phillip into the wall and he screamed. His rage was overtaking him and he didn't even try to stop it. He wanted all of it to come out and for the world to see it. "You will pay and nothing is going to help you. Not your God, not anyone." Kevin then started to choke Phillip. He did it slowly so he could enjoy it. Phillip closed his eyes and started to cry. That wasn't going to stop Kevin; in fact, it just made his feel even better about it. He wanted Phillip to cry and beg for his life so he could tell him that he couldn't have it and then kill him.

"Now," said Kevin, "I bet you want to beg for your life, don't you?" Phillip could not speak but he shook his head to give Kevin an answer. Kevin couldn't believe it. Who did he think he was? He was in no kind of position to give an answer like that. He had no control over his life. Kevin did. At any moment Kevin could have ended it for him and all he could do was sit there and wait for it to happen. Kevin thought that he should just let him go and torment him some more, but what if that was what he wanted? Then Kevin would be doing nothing and Phillip would really be in control. *But what if he wanted a quick death?* thought Kevin. Soon after a long internal struggle, Kevin decided to talk to Phillip about it.

Kevin let him go and Phillip quickly crawled into the corner and wrapped himself into a ball, shaking.

"So what are you thinking now?" asked Kevin, sounding almost calm. Phillip didn't respond he just kept shaking. "Did you just want me to finish you off quickly or are you still fighting for your life?" Still there was no answer. "YOU WILL ANSWER ME!" yelled Kevin as he kicked Phillip's desk. It went sliding in Phillip's direction and almost hit him. A loud, strident scream escaped Phillip's throat as he watched the wall he was leaning against being pierced by his desk.

"So now you're scared! What did you think would happen when you answered me like that? Did you think I would just kill you or did you want this to happen?" Phillip continued to scream and cry and didn't answer Kevin. He could not even hear what he was saying over his own voice. This made Kevin twice as angry. He quickly walked over to Phillip and picked him up again.

"What made you answer me like that," said Kevin, having to scream over him in order to be heard. Phillip was shaken by Kevin's voice and he quickly shut his mouth. He tried to stop crying, but he just couldn't stop himself.

"You are going to talk to me," said Kevin as he started to shake Phillip. He tried to keep his eyes closed as Kevin did this but he couldn't. His eyes opened almost automatically. Once his eyes were open they quickly looked past Kevin. There was a cloud behind him that was as white as snow. Phillip could see a light glow coming from it and he just looking at it seemed to ease his pain. He was about to say something when the cloud spoke instead. Kevin couldn't hear it.

"Don't say anything. I'm here to speak with you and only you. The man that is trying to kill you can't see or hear me. The Lord has blinded him, but not you. You are a liar and a cheater. You have no place in heaven and you don't deserve one. You belong in hell and deserve to burn among the demons. I can help you. I don't even think that this will be hard for you to do, but if you do it I will get God to spare your life and this man will not kill you. All you have to do is trust me." The cloud then started to transform into a blank sheet of paper. Soon the word "read" appeared in black at the top of the sheet. Then other words started to appear on the paper. These ones were different from the one at the top. Instead of being black they were red, but not just any red. They were the color of blood. To make it even worse they wrote out something that was just as atrocious.

Deny God or Die.

Phillip was shocked by the message. This was funny because he had been doing this his whole life, but now it felt wrong. He had just been trying to make a living and had never really thought about what could happen if he said those words. Now it terrified him and his eye lids opened so wide that his eyes could have fallen out.

"What are you doing now?" asked Kevin as he looked into Phillip's face. The expression on his face even scared Kevin. He thought that he had either already died or that there was something else that he was afraid of. Kevin put his ear against his nose and could hear him breathing. He was relieved but he still didn't know what was wrong.

"What are you looking at? Talk to me!" Phillip was no longer concerned with Kevin. He was fighting himself to keep from saying those words. His mouth seemed to be fixed on saying lies and wanted so badly to say this one. He was using all of his energy to control himself, but he was slowly slipping. His mind and body seemed to be somewhere else and all he had left was his soul. This was the one thing that he had control of and was fighting for. He had read enough of the scriptures to know that even if he somehow made it to heaven that he had done nothing that was righteous and good and there would be no treasure waiting for him. The image of him being a slave and unimportant continued to flash in his head. He felt so confused and didn't have a clue of what he should do. He knew that one way or the other he was going to die today and that there was nothing he could do about that. At first he thought that he should just deny God and see what would happen. Then he thought that if there was a God then he would burn in hell even if he was able to live on the earth for a little while longer. But what if there wasn't one and someone had just made all of the theology up and it was inane. Then there would be no point in his dying for nothing and he should just give in to what ever wanted him to deny God. Though there were many choices, there wasn't much time and he had to make a choice fast. One way or the other he had lived a life that he wasn't proud of and wished that he could change. What could he do now?

"NO," said Phillip. "I can't do that. I will not."

"What are you talking about?" asked Kevin. "You will answer me and there in nothing you can do about that! I am in control here."

"No," said Phillip as he quickly started to shake his head from side to side. His head was moving so fast that it was hard for Kevin to see his face.

"What is wrong with you?" asked Kevin, sounding a little frightened. He had no idea of what was going on. "I want to know what is going on and you will answer me." Phillip just continued to shake his head and nothing came out of his mouth. Now his head was moving so fast that usually it would have fallen off along time ago, but some anonymous vigor was keeping it from doing that. Kevin couldn't take much more of this and by now he was afraid that he might not still be in control.

"If you don't answer me I will kill you," said Kevin, trying to sound as if he had some kind of authority.

"I will die either way," said Phillip, still shaking his head.

"Okay," said Kevin, raising his hand, "it's time for you to—"

But Phillip cut him off. "No!" screamed Phillip. Then a bright white illumination came out of his eyes. Kevin had never seen such a bright radiance. He wanted to run, but he didn't see why he should. He raised his hand and smiled as he released the power that he had inside of it. He thought that it would have pierced through the illumination, but he was wrong. The illumination, instead, consumed Kevin's power and grew stronger. Kevin didn't know what to do and he didn't have much time to think. Before he could do much of anything else a beam came out of the white illumination and hit him. He was lucky that he couldn't feel much of anything because this is a blow that no one would want to feel. He was sent flying through the wall that was behind him and out into the street. Kevin found himself in the church parking lot and he quickly got to his feet. He was amazed that something like that had happened to him. He couldn't believe that something had enough power to do that to him. Phillip interrupted his thoughts.

"No," said Phillip, floating in the white light towards Kevin. "Now I have the power and I will kill him. You will not stop me. You earned this." Phillip continued to get closer and closer to Kevin. Kevin just sat there. He was certain that Phillip had gone crazy and was talking to nothing. Kevin wasn't just going to stand around and allow Phillip to have control of everything.

"That was a good shot," said Kevin, raising his hand, "now it's my turn." Kevin them released even more of his power and knocked Phillip out of the air. Phillip slid on the concrete for a few moments and then stopped suddenly. Kevin was almost scared to walk over and look at him. While he was trying to decide the old lady appeared.

"Hurry up, Kevin," said the old lady, raising his hand. "He has to die quickly."

"Okay," said Kevin, allowing the woman to take control of him. "I want him to die. He has gotten on my nerves for the last time." Then Kevin raised his hand and fired one last shot. This shot had sent dust into the air and Kevin had to wait for it all to settle down before he had a chance to see if Phillip had survived. He saw nothing and was content. He did not know why, but he felt as if a heavy burden had been taken from him and he no longer had any worries. He wasn't sure if he should just stand there or leave. He didn't even feel like himself anymore. It was as if he had been reborn and was a new person.

"Kevin," said the old lady from out of the sky, "you need to get out of here, now."

"Yes, okay," said Kevin as he turned to walk away. He walked over to his car and got in. He didn't know where he should go and then a picture of Samantha appeared in his head. His anger suddenly came back and he could barely control himself. He was going to make her suffer for what she had put him through. He was going to make her feel all of the pain that he had felt and more. It was time for her to die.

Kevin made it to his house a few minutes later. Samantha's car was in the driveway and he wasn't sure if he should be happy or sad about that. When he got out the car he was hoping that his children weren't home, but then he thought to himself that it really didn't matter. They were going to find out anyways and if they were there it would only make it easier for them to believe. Kevin took one last breath and then opened the door to his house.

"Samantha," yelled Kevin as he took his first step into the house. "Where are you?"

"Kevin," yelled Samantha from somewhere inside of the house, "is that you? Where have you been all of this time? I've been so worried. Are you okay?" Samantha had been walking towards him all of this time and now Kevin could see her. He almost wanted to just lunge out at her and choke her until she could no longer breathe, but he constrained himself.

"How are you, Samantha?" asked Kevin with an evil smile on his face.

"What do you mean how am I? How are you and where did you go? You are in no condition to just be going around as you please. What if something happened to you? What would I do then?"

"I don't know. Why don't you tell me?" said Kevin as he walked past her into the living room.

"What do you mean?" asked Samantha, sounding very shocked, but Kevin was sure that she knew what he was talking about.

"Are the children home?"

"No. Why?" Samantha was starting to feel a little afraid, but she just kept telling herself that she had been in much worse circumstances than this.

"I have a few things I need to talk to you about. These questions must be answered, or bad things might happen."

"Kevin, I think you've taken to much medicine," said Samantha, backing out of the room. "I'll go and get something to help you."

"No," said Kevin, reaching out and grabbing her. "You will stay here and speak with me." Kevin then lifted her off of the ground and threw her on the couch. Samantha was terrified now and she didn't know what else to do but sit there and talk.

"What do you want to talk about?" asked Samantha, getting angry with Kevin.

"Watch your voice," said Kevin. "We can do this without animosity between us."

"Well, let us hurry up then."

"Okay, I need...I need—" Kevin then stopped what he was saying. He wasn't sure of what he was going to say. What did he want to know? Then Carlos popped into his head and Robert and everything that had been haunting him over the last few days. He just didn't know where to start.

"What did you do to Carlos?" asked Kevin, looking right in Samantha's face.

"What are you talking about?" asked Samantha, trying to get off of the couch, but Kevin quickly pushed her back down.

"I'm talking about the man you killed and hid in my parents' old house. Why did you do it?"

"Kevin, what do you mean? Are you talking about that Carlos that used to go to my church? I already told you about him."

"Samantha, why do you do this to me? I loved you with all of my heart. You could have told me what really happened to Robert."

"What happened to Robert? What are you talking about? He died and there is nothing else to it."

"Why must you lie to me? I gave you everything and anything you wanted whether I could get it or not. What do you think Phillip is going to do for you?"

"Phillip?" asked Samantha as she got up from the couch and started to pull something out of her back pocket. "I don't know what you are talking about. Kevin, you need to lie down for a while and calm down."

"What do you mean? Are you telling me that everything that has happened was fake?"

"I think so, honey. So just calm down."

"I don't believe you," said Kevin, grabbing Samantha's shoulders and pulling her close to him. "Tell me the truth!"

"I don't think that matters," said Samantha as she pulled the knife out of her pocket and stabbed Kevin in the chest. Kevin had seen it coming and was going to block it when he thought it was not going to hurt him, but soon the pain came and Kevin fell to the ground. This pain was greater than anything he had ever felt and he couldn't bear it. Not only had she stabbed him but she had also broken his heart. He had tried hard to believe her and he was going to until she stabbed him.

Once he was on the ground Samantha didn't wait another minute to knock Kevin in the head and try to make him unconscious. Kevin just took the blows and lay there heartbroken. Up until this moment Kevin had never really thought that his love for Samantha would disappear. He had thought that some how it was going to be saved and they would learn to love each other again, but he was wrong.

Samantha continued to hit him until she thought he was knocked out and then she looked in his face.

"You are a fool," said Samantha as she spat in his face not knowing that he was conscious. "All this time I have just been using you. Ever since we first meet I've been cheating on you and doing things behind your back. I killed Robert and his father. It wasn't my fault though; his father just wanted him and wouldn't allow him to be raised by you. I knew that you would never allow something like that and after I killed his father I saw no more use for him so he had to die. You're lucky that Keith's father really didn't care. Don't worry though, the rest are all yours. Yes I did kill Carlos. I had to; he was going to mess up everything for me. Phillip and I are going to go places. Well at least I am. Once I'm finished with him I'll probably kill him also. I know you're surprised but it will be okay in the end. You will go to wherever you're meant to go and I'll be with God."

Samantha then spat in his face and again and started to laugh. Kevin did not have much strength left, but he wasn't just going to lie there and let her get away with something like this. Kevin reached up and grabbed her throat and said, "You will die now." Samantha stabbed Kevin's hand and he let her go, but it was too late. Blood began to come out of Samantha. It came from her mouth and her ears and her nose. Everywhere there was a hole in her body there was blood pushing its way out. Samantha didn't last long and soon her body was motionless on the floor next to Kevin. Kevin wanted to laugh at her, but he was too weak. He did enjoy watching her die, but he didn't know what he could do for himself. He tried to think of healing himself, but he had too much of a headache to think straight. All he could do lie down and die.

"Are you okay, Kevin?" asked the old lady, standing over him.

"What do you think?" asked Kevin very quietly.

"Well, why don't you heal yourself?"

"I can't. I'm too weak."

"So do you need my help?"

"Yes, please help me."

"Do you trust me?"

"Yes...help me?" Kevin then fainted. Before this happened though he had given his entire soul to the old lady. Everything that was inside of him belonged to her and now there was almost no way of getting it all back. Kevin was hers to do whatever she wanted with and there was nothing he could do. He would do as she pleased without complaining and he would have no say in what happened. He had fallen into her trap and now there was no one who could help him. Well there was one thing that would have set him free, but that was something he would find out later. The old woman's plan was working as she had planned and now it was time for it to advance further. Kevin was now completely lost and he would have to work twice as hard to find himself again.

An hour later, Keith's friend brought him home. He had been waiting for his mother to come and get him, but she never came. He figured that she must have just forgotten about him, but he never expected to find what he did. His house was gone. All that was left was ash. He didn't know what to do. An impulse told him to run. He didn't know what he was running to or what for, but he just had to run.

He was running so fast that a cop almost didn't notice him as he ran past him towards the house. Keith had almost made it to the house when Detective Roy stopped him. Keith hadn't realized it but he had been crying this whole time.

"Hey, are you okay?" asked Roy, looking into his face. "You're one of his children, aren't you?" Keith just stood there crying. "Yes, you're the older one, aren't you? Your name is Keith I believe." Keith just nodded his head to say yes and then looked down. They both just sat there for a while and then Keith spoke.

"What happened?"

"We don't know. All we know it that someone started a fire and only one person died."

"Who was it?" asked Keith, still looking at the ground.

"It was...your mother."

"It was her...alone."

"Yes."

"Where are my brothers?"

"There over by my car. They're fine, you don't have to worry."

"Where is my father?"

"We don't know. We can't find him."

"Could he be in there also?"

"Yes, he could. We're still looking, but let's not hope for the worst."

"What could be worse?"

"Keith, I know this is hard for you. My parents died when I was much younger than you, but I didn't let that kill me. Will you allow me to invite you to my house to stay the night?"

"I don't see why not. No one's around to say I can't."

"It's going to be okay," said Roy, embracing Keith. Keith usually wouldn't have allowed such a thing, but now it didn't matter much. He couldn't believe something like this was happening. He wasn't worried about Kevin. If he was dead then he would get over that, but Samantha was the one he was worried about. He had so many questions to ask her about his father. She would never know that he had found out the truth, and from Keith's point of view neither would

Kevin. Keith couldn't help but think that his father had done this for revenge on Samantha. Hatred was building in his heart and there was almost nothing he could do about it.

"Keith, we can't stay out here all night," said Roy, starting to lead him towards his car. As they walked Keith saw both of his brothers crying in front or Roy's police car.

"Keith," said Roy, opening the door for his brothers to get into the back seat.

"Yes, Detective."

"I have many things I need to talk to you about. I know that it will be hard for you, but these things must be answered. I'll wait until we get to my house and we are alone before I start to talk to you.

"Okay," said Keith, getting into the car. "I'm all yours." Then Roy got into the car and they started to drive off. Keith looked back at the house one last time and started to feel anger towards Kevin. He couldn't explain it. He just wanted to kill him. He felt as if that was his only mission in life and he wasn't going to allow anything to stop him. His anger was so great that if he had known Kevin was only a few blocks away inside of an abandoned house he would have done anything to get a hold of him and kill him.

If only someone would have reached out and truly told them about Jesus, maybe then none of this would have ever happened. Though many people tried, they never lived up to the things that would have allowed them to truly reach these people. This is such a horrid story and I would stop, but in order for it to be understood the rest must be told. Farewell for now, but Kevin's story will be told. The touch will be used.

Printed in the United Kingdom
by Lightning Source UK Ltd.
127892UK00001B/90/A